FROM THE BLACK HILLS

FROM THE BLACK HILLS

JUDY TROY

RANDOM HOUSE NEW YORK

Grateful acknowledgment is made to Sony/ATV Music Publishing for
permission to reprint an excerpt from "Hello Walls" by Willie Nelson.
Copyright © 1961 by Sony/ATV Songs LLC (renewed).
All rights administered by Sony/ATV Music Publishing,
8 Music Square West, Nashville, TN 37203.
Reprinted by permission.

Troy, Judy
From the Black Hills / Judy Troy.
p.   cm.
ISBN 0-375-50230-0 (alk. paper)
I. Title.
PS3570.R68F76   1999
813'.54—dc21   98-53465

Random House website address: www.atrandom.com
Printed in the United States of America on acid-free paper
2 4 6 8 9 7 5 3
First Edition
Book design by Jo Anne Metsch

FOR MILLER AND HARDY

ACKNOWLEDGMENTS

With gratitude to the Whiting Foundation; to Bob Overturf at the Division of Criminal Investigation in Rapid City, whose help was invaluable; to Frank Walters for his motorcycle wisdom; to Robin Bernstein for his beautiful sentence; and to Georges and Anne Borchardt for, among other things, their faith in me.

I would also like to thank Mark Siegert for his inestimable help and support; Mary D. Kierstead, always; Miller Solomon, for more than I can say; Jeanne Tift; Beth Pearson; Margaret Wimberger; and Daniel Menaker, whose intelligence and talent have now graced my work a second time.

FROM THE BLACK HILLS

PROLOGUE

Early Sunday morning in the third week of August, Michael Newlin left Wheatley, South Dakota, for college. His mother stood in the driveway alone, in her church clothes, to see him off. Behind her was the two-story brick house he'd grown up in, which she would live in by herself now. His father had been missing for more than eight weeks. On June 18, without having done a violent thing ever before, he had shot and killed Mary Hise, the young woman who'd worked as receptionist at his small insurance agency. Then he'd disappeared. He'd been seen in Kansas, but that was back in July. By this time he could be any-where.

"Concentrate on your own life now," Mike's mother said. She was almost as tall as he was, her short hair blown back by the dry wind. She kissed him through the open window of his pickup, and he backed down the driveway, drove down Edge Street, and turned onto the interstate.

South Dakota State University, in Brookings, was over four hundred miles east, not far from the Minnesota state line. It would take him seven hours to get there. He'd brought cassettes to listen to, including one that his girlfriend, Donetta Rush, had made for him.

"Don't listen to it until you're on the highway," she'd asked him the night before. "You have to promise." He'd promised, and then he'd listened to the beginning of it on his way home from her house.

The first thing on the cassette was her voice. "It's three o'clock in the morning," she said. "I can't sleep, I can't dream, and I can't stop thinking of you."

"Miss You," by the Rolling Stones, was the first song.

PART I

WHEATLEY

ONE

IN the spring of Mike's senior year, months before graduation, he was working long hours at Neil Schofield's cattle ranch. He was bored with school, and Josh Mitchell, his closest friend, had moved to Wyoming in February, with his father, after his parents' divorce. Josh's mother was with somebody else now.

Mike had worked at the Schofield ranch every summer since he was fourteen, and this year, in March, he began working mornings before school, getting up in the dark and riding his motorcycle—bought despite his parents' objections—out on Route 8 through the cold dawn. On those days he ate breakfast with the Schofields—with Neil, his wife, Lee-Ann, and their two-year-old daughter, Janna. Often Neil's brother, Ed, who lived in Buffalo Gap, would be there, too, having driven over in his old Corvette. He was an artist; he made pottery that he sold in Rapid City. Two other men, Arthur Strong and Louis Ivy, showed up after breakfast. They looked older than they were, and neither of them could read very well. If they got there early, they waited outside, next to their pickups.

"I can make you breakfast here," Mike's mother had offered. "I'm up early anyway." She taught high school biology and did her class preparations in the mornings before school.

"I don't mind eating with the Schofields," Mike had told her, not saying that he preferred it to being home. The previous summer, when Mike had left home for the ranch before sunrise and not come back before nine at night, he'd said that he liked being alone on the tractor, listening to his father's old rock-and-roll tapes on his Walkman. He'd kept quiet about Neil Schofield, whose first two strikes against him, according to Mike's father, were that he was rich and hadn't had to work for it. Neil's wealthy father had bought the ranch for his retirement. Now he lived in California, and Neil ran the ranch for real, sort of. He could hire as many people as he needed and could afford having bad luck. "Money just doesn't mean that much to me," he'd told Mike.

"Let's see," Mike had said once. "If I work half an hour longer, I can afford to buy Donetta popcorn tonight at the movies." Neil had given him an extra twenty dollars with that week's pay. "I'm bullshitting you," Mike had had to explain.

Neil was fifteen years younger than Mike's father. He was tall, light-haired, and energetic, and in good shape from his work on the ranch. Mike's father, Glenn, was of average height, thin, and dark-haired, and had never been particularly happy. What Mike told himself most often was that his father had gotten lost trying to find what other people already had. Glenn didn't have the key, somehow. Mike felt that his father was always trying to figure out how he'd come into being, and how Mike had come into being, what point there was to it and how you were supposed to get through your life. Once, late one night, when Mike's mother was away, Mike had heard his father cry for almost an hour. In the morning neither of them had mentioned it. His father had never hit Mike—or anyone else, as far as Mike knew—but he got his feelings hurt too easily. And when he got angry it turned into a dark mood that lasted a long time, often weeks. "Mr. Gloom," Mike would refer to him as then, but only to himself. It would be too disloyal to use this kind of nickname, even with Josh and Donetta. Anyway, his father wasn't always like that.

Something else Mike kept quiet about with everyone were his feelings for Lee-Ann Schofield. When he first knew her, when he was fourteen, she had teased him about some things he'd mentioned to Neil, such as getting into trouble with Josh, drunk at the bowling alley, or sneaking out at three in the morning to throw eggs at somebody's window. But over the years she'd teased him less and talked to him more. She was thirteen years older than he was, thirty the year he turned seventeen. Mike was tall by then—not as tall as Neil but taller than his father, and muscular from high school wrestling and working on the ranch. He'd let his dark hair grow as long as he could before his coach objected. He looked more like his mother's side of the family: green eyes, a long face, high cheekbones.

Lee-Ann had small, pretty features. Her brown hair was unevenly cut—collar-length in back, shorter around her face. In the sunlight, Mike noticed, her hair had shades of gold and red. She wore loose clothes and no makeup and seemed to have a private way she felt about herself that was different from what other people thought they knew about her. That was what Mike liked about her. She was secretive, the way he was.

On an October morning of Mike's senior year, he went into the Schofields' house for a Coke just as Lee-Ann was coming into the kitchen after a shower. In the half second before she belted her thin robe, he saw her breasts, her stomach—a fleshiness that the girls he knew didn't have; they dieted and ran and lifted weights. Even Lee-Ann's face was softer, and seemed capable of gentler expressions. After that day, with her wet face and hair, her open robe, and the way she'd looked at him when she saw him looking at her, Mike became more sexual around her. He didn't think about the age difference anymore and hardly thought of her as married. In his mind he separated her from Neil and from his friendship with Neil.

By the time winter came, the moment he saw her was the moment he came to count on most, though he couldn't have said for what, or why. Because, as his advanced-placement English teacher would have said—she was always making them read stories about people who weren't lucky—his life was a lucky one: a nice-enough house, responsible parents, the ability to get good grades. And even that left out something: Donetta having sex with him on weekend nights at Crow Lake. Yet Mike couldn't change the way he felt about Lee-Ann Schofield; it was a fact, to him, rather than something he might question.

Instead, he fantasized about her all winter and spring. She was on his mind as he sat in class, watching snow fall on the field outside the window; as he rode his motorcycle too fast on the first warm days when the trees were budding; as he had sex with Donetta in the backseat of his mother's car. And at night in his house—his mother up late, grading papers in the dining room, his father in front of the television in the den—he lay in bed in the dark and masturbated, imagining that moment in the kitchen with Lee-Ann and picturing her robe coming off. His goal became to masturbate one day in her empty house—the emptiness sexual to him, somehow, as if his own body could fill all that space.

He didn't have the nerve or opportunity to do it until an

afternoon in late May, when Lee-Ann and Janna were in town and Neil had driven over to Ed's house in Buffalo Gap. Mike had walked through the house, noticing two things he'd never noticed before: a photograph of Lee-Ann breast-feeding her daughter, and a white plaster cast of Lee-Ann's hand when she was a child, her name etched into it underneath. He walked upstairs to the bedroom she shared with Neil, with its white curtains and pale carpet. But a pair of Neil's boots were next to a chair in the corner, so Mike settled for the upstairs hallway, in sight of Lee-Ann's robe in the bathroom and the blue comforter on her bed. He leaned against the wall and unzipped his jeans, and afterward, using toilet paper to clean himself up, his legs were shaking. He wanted to do it again, almost immediately. But the house was reassuming its identity, which didn't include him. He felt like an intruder then. He went home that night without coming up to the house to say good-bye the way he usually did, and he didn't come for breakfast the next morning.

On Saturday Lee-Ann came into the barn to find him. "Are you mad at me? Did I do something I don't remember?"

"No," he told her. "It's me. I've been busy with school."

"I miss you," she said, in the sweet voice he'd heard her use only with Neil and Janna; it made tears come to his eyes. "It's all right," Lee-Ann said gently, and they put their arms around each other for the first time. She held him so closely that he had to pull back in order to kiss her.

But she stepped away then, and walked out of the barn. He didn't see her again until that evening, as he was leaving. She was watching him from the front yard.

After that were days at the ranch Mike had to miss because of finals, graduation, and then, on June 18—a hot, bright Thursday afternoon—because of what his father did.

TWO

MARY Hise died before the ambulance arrived. It was Neil who told Mike what had happened. Mike, on the riding lawn mower, circling the pond, with the sun low behind him, saw Neil walking toward him from the house. He looked so serious that for a moment Mike was afraid he was going to say, "I know you want to screw my wife." What he said instead was, "Let's go sit on the porch. I have to tell you something about your father."

Mary Hise was naked. She was lying in the bathroom doorway of room 14 at the Tenderly Motel, in Wausee—a motel Mike had been to twice with Donetta.

"Your mother wanted you to hear this from me," Neil said. "Not from the police. They're already at your house." He was sitting across from Mike on the screened-in porch, Janna's dolls scattered on the floor between them. "Your father and Mary met at the motel. They got there at one o'clock, and they were drinking. Afterward your father called an ambulance, then drove off in Mary's car." Neil looked at his watch. "It's been three hours since he made the call."

"Why her car?" Mike's mouth was so dry that it was hard for him to talk.

"I don't know. Maybe to buy him time. They didn't know who she was for a while. Her purse wasn't there." Neil stood and went into the kitchen; he came back with a glass of water that he handed to Mike. "Your father even left the gun behind," he said. "It was registered to him."

"It was my grandfather's," Mike said slowly. He looked down the hill, toward the pond. He could see the line between what he had mowed and what he hadn't. It looked as sharp and distinct as the edge of a razor.

Neil leaned forward, the chair creaking as he moved. "I know how hard it is to believe. It is for me, too. I thought, somehow they've got your father confused with somebody else. But they don't. It's not a mistake."

"I know," Mike said. But that sounded as if he knew more about his father and Mary Hise than he did. He didn't know anything. That was what he couldn't put into words—what it was like to discover that there were things you almost knew but didn't know. He looked away from Neil. He leaned down and picked up Janna's dolls. He put them one by one in her red toy box.

"Your mother wants me to drive you home," Neil said. "She doesn't want you on your motorcycle tonight."

"I'm all right."

"I'll drive you anyway. I promised her."

Neil turned toward Lee-Ann, whom Mike noticed for the first time. She was standing at the porch door with the baby in her arms. They were like a snapshot of normal life, Mike thought—something he knew he hadn't been a part of even before this happened, something he seemed cut off from now in a permanent way. "I'm sorry, Mike," she said.

FIVE minutes later Neil loaded Mike's motorcycle into the back of his pickup. Lee-Ann had come outside with them. "Call us," she told Mike. She set Janna down, put her arms around Mike, and hugged him. It was nothing like before; he knew it couldn't be. And that scared him almost as much as the news about his father had. What he needed was proof that she wanted to be with him. If he could have that, then he could handle everything else that was happening.

"Don't worry about work," Neil told him on the way home. "Come back when you're ready, or just come over and talk."

"Okay," Mike said.

The sun was sinking behind the Black Hills, which were just a few miles away. It was cooler there, and Mike thought about how you could ride up there and get lost for a while on the winding roads, though they all brought you back to Wheatley or Hill City or one of the other small towns. You could never get lost long enough to see what lost felt like. You could never just disappear.

"I can't believe this happened," Neil said.

He pulled up in front of Mike's house. There were five policemen standing in the yard. There were seven cars parked along the curb.

THREE

THEY asked him questions. Had he seen his father carry anything out to the car last night, or this morning? Some of his father's clothes were gone. Did he know that his father had been transferring savings into his parents' checking account and then withdrawing them? He might have as much as four thousand dollars with him. Why did his father have books about wilderness survival? They'd taken those out of the bookshelf and gone through them, even though Mike's mother, Carolyn, had said, "Glenn hasn't looked at those in fifteen years." Had Mike ever seen his father with another woman? Why did his father have a gun? Had Mike ever been afraid of his father? Did Mike love him?

That last question came from a special agent with the Division of Criminal Investigation in Rapid City. His name was Tom DeWitt; Mike knew him and his mother knew of

him. His brother lived in Wheatley and was a teacher, and
his nephew had been on Mike's wrestling team. Mike had
seen Tom DeWitt at meets and knew that he had a cabin
somewhere near Lead. Once, after a wrestling meet in
Rapid City, he had treated the team to pizza.

He sat with Mike on the small patio outside the kitchen
door. It was not quite dark. Mike's mother was sitting inside at the kitchen table with two of her friends, both female teachers. Mike only had to look to his right, through
the window, to see her distressed, anxious face. And so
when the special agent asked Mike if he loved his father,
Mike glanced at her and said uneasily, "I guess I do. What
difference does it make?"

"I'm trying to get a picture of your father. I want to understand him."

"Why?"

"So I can think like him." Tom DeWitt crossed his legs,
his left ankle resting on his right knee. His intelligence
made Mike nervous. He wasn't expecting it. He'd grown
up seeing movies in which even smart policemen were
foolish in some ways. He wasn't sure that he could fool this
person, which made him wonder why he would think
about trying. Fool him about what?

"Am I your enemy or your friend?" he asked Mike.

"Neither."

"If your father contacted you, would you tell me?"

"I don't know."

The agent stood up to take off his suit jacket. He had

brown, thinning hair, narrow eyes, and a wide, relaxed-looking face. Under his jacket he was wearing a short-sleeved shirt. He worked out, Mike saw. He had large biceps and strong forearms. He was big-chested for his height. He lay his jacket across his lap. "I've seen you wrestle," he said. "Are you going to wrestle in college?"

"Not if it gets in the way of school."

"Is that you talking, or your parents?"

"I don't want to be some dumb-ass jock."

He laughed in such a friendly way that for a second Mike was confused about what the agent was there for, why he was talking to Mike. Mike looked through the window at his mother.

"Did your father watch you wrestle?" Tom DeWitt asked.

"Yes. He just didn't come every time."

"Why not?"

"Why should he?"

"I don't know. Some fathers would."

"I didn't expect him to," Mike said.

"Some fathers would go regardless."

"Well, he wasn't one of them."

"What kind was he, then?"

"Why should I describe him to you?" Mike said.

"Why shouldn't you?"

"Because you don't give a shit about him."

"He killed a twenty-four-year-old woman," the agent said.

"He called an ambulance," Mike said. "He wished he hadn't done it. He didn't want her to die."

"But she did die."

In the silence that followed, Mike could hear the cicadas, which sounded to him too harsh and too loud. He wasn't perceiving things right. The backyard seemed larger than it was; his mother, in the kitchen, seemed smaller and older. He had changed, too. He felt that he was looking at himself through unfocused binoculars. Yet the agent remained solid and whole. He seemed casual, even, until he said, "Do you think he's being blamed for something he didn't do?"

"Do you?"

"I'm not his son. I don't know what I'd think if I were."

"Because you know your father could never have done it."

"No. Anybody could do it."

"I couldn't," Mike said, and knew right away that he'd made a mistake. "That's not true," he said then. "I don't know what I could or couldn't do." He moved his hair out of his eyes. His hands were shaking. "I'm tired," he said. "I don't want to talk anymore."

Tom DeWitt stood up slowly, as if he were the tired one. He walked into the kitchen behind Mike, said good night to Mike's mother—one of her friends was leaving as well— and said good-bye to Mike. He looked once more at the pile of survival books before disappearing into the front part of the house. Mike didn't hear the door close, although from his room upstairs, which faced the street, he saw him cross the yard and get into a light-colored car.

Mike wasn't alone for more than a minute before his mother was standing in the doorway in her brown dress. That summer she was teaching part-time at the community college, and she was still in her teaching clothes.

"Ms. Watkins is spending the night with us," she told Mike. Noleen Watkins, who dated Mike's wrestling coach, had been Mike's seventh-grade social studies teacher; she'd taken his class on a field trip to Badlands National Park. His mother sometimes referred to her friends at school by their last names, even younger women like Noleen. "You've spent too much time in school, Carolyn," Mike's father used to tell her. "Everybody is Mr. or Mrs. So-and-So."

"Mr. or Ms.," his mother would say sharply, ignoring the point his father had been making. She was good at that, Mike knew. She never thought that people's responses had anything to do with her, with how she acted or what she said. Mike had seen her do that at school, too. For four years he'd had to see her there in addition to at home. While she'd kept track of his behavior, his grades, and his friends, he'd kept track of her, too—of how she could ignore an unhappy student or snub an entire class that didn't like her. In the end that changed the way Mike felt about her. Before that, she'd been his friend. She'd helped him with his homework. She'd driven him and Josh to Rapid City for baseball games.

Now she shut Mike's door behind her, crossed the room, and stood with him at the open window. "Did Tom De-

Witt tell you anything?" she asked. "Do you think they know where he is?"

"He just asked questions," Mike said. The night had grown windy. Mike could hear it in the chimes that hung from the front porch, below his room. His father had bought them for his mother a long time ago. His father had paid for them, but Mike had picked them out.

"You should eat something," his mother said. "There's meat loaf, and macaroni and cheese." When Mike didn't respond, she touched his arm. "Even if you don't feel hungry."

"I don't."

"Sit down with me." She sat on the bed and waited for Mike to sit next to her. "Your father and Mary Hise were having an affair," she told him. "It started last fall, or in the winter. I'm not sure. I didn't know until three weeks ago." Her voice had become unsteady, and she began to cry. Mike looked down at the brown carpeting, then at the closed door. Finally, he put his arms around her—something he'd never done before unless he was hugging her hello or good-bye. He felt how thin she was, thinner than she looked.

After a few moments she sat up straight and dried her face. "I'm all right," she said. "You know that. I'm not the kind of person who falls apart."

Like Dad, Mike thought. He moved over a little, so that there was a few inches of space between them.

"Mary Hise told Dad she was quitting," his mother

said. "That was toward the end of May, when you weren't home much."

"I wanted to make money for college."

"I know. I'm not criticizing you." She took a deep breath. She looked at Mike's closet and so did he—the door to it open, his jeans and work shirts stacked neatly on the shelves. "Dad was distraught," she said. "He would hardly talk. He couldn't sleep. Finally I called Mary Hise and asked her to meet me for coffee, and she said yes. We met at Shoney's. I said, 'You and Glenn are having an affair,' as if I already knew, because I was sure. And she said, 'We were having an affair, but that's in the past. That's why I'm leaving. He still wants—' " Carolyn stopped and turned her head at a noise in the hallway—Noleen Watkins closing the bathroom door. Mike had already forgotten that she was there, that she was staying overnight. Then his mother said, "I hate telling you these things. I hate for you to know them."

"Well, you know them," Mike said.

"I'm not eighteen. I'm not his child." When Mike started to protest, she said, "You're not a child anymore. I know that." She seemed to focus on the Grateful Dead poster taped to the wall above his bed. Donetta had bought it for him a year ago—what seemed to Mike now like a hundred years ago.

"Dad didn't want Mary Hise to leave," his mother said. "I told her, 'Just stay in the job a little longer, until he gets used to the idea of your leaving. Wait until he calms down.' " She turned toward Mike as if he'd spoken. "What would you expect me to say? I was afraid your father was going to kill himself."

She didn't have to explain why; Mike already knew. His father had tried to kill himself once before, twenty-some years before, during his freshman year at the University of South Dakota. He'd been dating Mike's mother's roommate, and when she had broken up with him he'd taken an overdose of pills—tranquilizers of some kind. "Things were different then," Mike's mother had told Mike once. "Vietnam was going on. People talked about death and suicide. I felt compassionate toward your father. He was more sensitive than the other boys I knew."

Mike had seen an old picture of his parents: the two of them sitting on the grass in front of a classroom building, his mother's hair waist-length and his father's almost to his shoulders. It had been taken the spring of their sophomore year, by which time they were a couple—his father the handsome one and his mother the smart one. It seemed to Mike that they'd stayed the same in that way, except that his father's expression had changed, had become bewildered, Mike thought, or hopeless.

"You know as much as I do about the rest," his mother said. "Mary stayed on. Your father seemed calmer. I didn't know they were still involved. I didn't know she'd lied to me. I thought that she'd quit before long, and then your dad and I would—I don't know. Talk about it." She looked down at her hands. The only ring she wore was her wedding band.

"Did Dad know you knew?"

"No. I don't think so."

"Did you tell the police you knew?"

"Of course. I had to." She got up and closed Mike's curtains. "When you're married a long time . . ." she said. Then, "Dad and I weren't . . ." She turned toward him. "Marriages are complicated. All of them are." Her eyes were teary. "Are you all right?" she asked. "Do you think you can sleep?"

Mike nodded. She stood next to the door for a moment, before opening it, and Mike thought about how many nights she'd done that during his life—not nights like this but ordinary ones, when she'd come in to say good night, then stand there as if she couldn't bring herself to leave. He used to count the seconds to himself until he could be free of her. Although there was a time, when he was much younger, when he hadn't minded it; sometimes he had liked it. That was hard for him to remember now.

"I'll see you in the morning," she said. "Things will seem clearer when we've gotten some sleep."

She opened the door, and he listened to her footsteps in the hall, his heart beating fast. He knew too many private things, and now he knew more. He'd known that his parents weren't happy with each other. He'd known that his father was never going to be happy with anyone. He'd known, even, that there had been something wrong with his father lately, but that hadn't been the only time he'd felt that. If you felt something often enough, you hardly felt it anymore. You were so used to certain things being wrong that you didn't ask questions. You stopped wondering. You just told yourself that everything was the way it always was.

He could hear thunder in the west, over the Black Hills, or even farther away, in Wyoming. He turned off the light, sat on his bed, and thought about Mary Hise. She had been his father's receptionist for a year and a half; she'd had red hair and dark eyes. Mike hadn't known her well. One afternoon in December, at his father's office, he had spoken to her for just a few minutes. They'd talked about her dog, Harrison. "In warm weather I take him out to Little Falls Park after dinner," she'd said. "I ride my bike, and he runs behind me." She showed Mike a picture of herself with the tan dog at her feet. Part cocker spaniel, she had said. She'd put the picture back in her desk drawer. She'd stopped talking when Mike's father walked over.

Mike had seen her once, the previous summer, at the public pool. In a bikini, she'd looked sexier than he would have imagined. She'd had bigger breasts than he would have thought. Mike had been at the pool with Donetta; he'd not spoken to Mary Hise, but he remembered how she looked. He was uncomfortable now—ashamed, even, of recalling so clearly what her body was like. It didn't seem believable that she was dead.

Lightning lit up his room, and rain began to fall. When he looked out the window there was only a minute before the Hylers' house across the street became impossible to see. Their place was a disaster, anyway—an old frame house with peeling paint and a second-floor porch in danger of caving in. In the front yard was an oak tree over a hundred years old. The Hylers were almost that old themselves. It was Donetta's favorite house in Wheatley, and not for its potential to be fixed up, either. She liked it the way it was—almost condemned. "If you lived in it," she'd say, "you'd feel that your life was part of history."

Mike went downstairs and opened the kitchen door. It was after midnight. It was raining so hard that he couldn't see beyond the patio to the neatly mown lawn, which was his job to keep up, or to the garbage cans in the alley, which were his responsibility, too—to take out the garbage and move the cans back up the driveway between pickup days. His mother kept things clean inside, as he did outside. What were his father's jobs? Mike wondered now. There was a workbench in the carport, which Mike had seen him use only a few times. Did something happen to people who didn't have routine, everyday things to do?

Mike hadn't eaten since noon. He closed the back door, opened the refrigerator, and took out the meat loaf, which he ate cold, standing up. Then he put it back and climbed the stairs. The rooms were dark. His mother's door was closed; the door to the guest room wasn't shut completely. He could see the shape of Noleen Watkins in bed. He stood there until his eyes adjusted to the darkness; then he could see that the bedsheet was thrown back, and that she had on a sleeveless nightgown. He wasn't attracted to her; she was a teacher he'd liked but never had a crush on, yet in the dark hallway he couldn't stop looking at her. Because he was a bad person, he thought—capable of any terrible thing.

Back in his room, he sat at his desk. In front of him was a stack of notebooks from his senior year that he hadn't gotten rid of yet; a pencil sketch of himself that Donetta had drawn, which said, on the back, "I love you forever"; and his acceptance letter to the honors program at South Dakota State University. That was all from the life he used to have, which now seemed shallow and unimportant. He hadn't been serious enough. He hadn't been paying enough attention to what was going on around him. He hadn't realized how much of your life could just come apart.

He lay down and tried to sleep. The rain outside hadn't let up. When he did fall asleep he woke twice from dreams in which his father, stranded in a storm, with the police after him, felt desperate enough to kill himself—this time for real. After the second dream Mike sat up and turned on his lamp. All right, he told himself. That's how I would feel. But how would Dad feel?

Misunderstood, Mike thought. He was able to sleep a little then. Years later he would realize how ironic that was, to find that comforting.

FOUR

IN the morning there was an unmarked police car parked across the street. The sky was overcast, and the storm had torn things up. Mike would have to pick up the fallen oak branches and the pieces of his mother's ceramic bird feeder, which he'd heard break in the night. Next door, Clyde Pate, old as he was, was up on his roof with a push broom.

Mike was standing at the window, watching him, when Donetta drove up. She walked across the yard to the back of the house, barefoot, wearing her blue uniform from Andell's Diner. Seeing her, Mike felt more able to go down to the kitchen and face his mother and Noleen Watkins. What ruined it was that when he walked into the kitchen, Donetta said, "Honey"—as if they were married, he thought, as if what his father had done had given her some kind of right to him.

She jumped up and hugged him; then she got him a glass of juice and brought it to where he stood, leaning stiffly against the farthest counter. He knew he was being a jerk; he felt that he was entitled to be anything he wanted to be today.

"Don't you have to be at work in a few minutes?" he asked her. He saw his mother frown at him.

"I am going to work," Donetta said. "I tried to get off, but Mr. Andell said no, he couldn't replace me."

Mr. Asshole, Mike thought, correcting her in his head. That was what Donetta would have called him any other day, even in front of his mother. Andell's Diner was just outside Wheatley, off the interstate—a truck stop, really, though no one in town called it that.

"I even have to work an extra shift," Donetta said in an offended way. She went back to the table and stood behind his mother and Noleen Watkins.

Mike stayed where he was, looking down at his juice glass, knowing that he'd become the center of attention. He couldn't tell if they expected him to do something crazy, or to do some take-control, you're-the-man-now kind of thing.

"I cancelled my classes for today and tomorrow," his mother said to him. She was in her nightgown and robe. "I'll go back Monday. Can Neil Schofield do without you for a few days?"

"I don't think so," Mike said. "I might have to help him out today or tomorrow." He tried to look right at her as he spoke, but it was hard. He was more used to telling half-truths and leaving things out than he was to lying outright. But he had to see Lee-Ann sooner than Monday. Monday was too far away. If he could just see her, he thought, then he could keep her inside his head and keep what was happening outside.

"All right," his mother said. He could see how tired she was then, probably even more tired than he was, and he almost gave in to the impulse to be nicer. What stopped him were his mother, Noleen Watkins, and Donetta lined up there like that at the table—against him, he felt, treating him like all of a sudden he might be a different person.

"It's probably better for Mike to stay busy," Noleen said. She said it so kindly that Mike's anger just left him. He sat down and let Donetta take his hand.

"I just wanted you to have company this morning," Donetta told him shyly, and that made her seem more like herself again to Mike. She understood how he felt—partly because they were alike. She had told him, as early as their first date, that he was the only person who'd ever made her feel less alone. "Alone in what way?" Mike had asked. "Alone as a person," she'd said, and he'd felt that she was talking about him, even though she'd been talking about herself.

They were both more themselves when he walked her outside to her car. "I can't believe this shit," Donetta said. "I can't believe this is real."

They were standing next to her silver Geo, in view of the

policeman parked across the street, looking at the house through his open window. Donetta put her arms around Mike's neck. She was small and small-boned; she had long hair streaked blond at the beauty school her mother owned. She was a year behind Mike in school. "That cop is watching us," Mike told her.

"I know," Donetta said, and she put her hand down the front of his jeans for just an instant as she kissed him. After she left, there was just Mike and the policeman, the empty street between them, and Donetta's silver car speeding away twice as fast as it should have.

"She's late for work," Mike said to the officer as offhandedly as he could before walking across the soaked grass toward the house. He picked up branches from the oak tree his father had planted the year he was born, and he picked up pieces of his mother's bird feeder. He knew that the policeman was probably watching him, and he felt as if he were in a movie, acting the part of a criminal's guilty son, even though he didn't know what he was guilty of.

Inside, he sat at the table with Noleen Watkins and ate a bowl of cereal. He felt uncomfortable alone with her. His mother had gone upstairs to dress. Noleen, in jeans and a pink shirt, her hair pulled back and her glasses hanging from a chain around her neck, was holding her coffee cup with both hands. "I haven't seen you in a long time," she told Mike. "Your mother says that you're going to South Dakota State in the fall."

"I was. I still am, I guess."

"I know how you must feel," she said. "But don't lose sight of your own plans."

"I won't," he said, to be polite. Outside, the sun broke through the clouds and streamed in through the window, filling the kitchen with light.

"It's easy to give advice, isn't it?" Noleen said. "Teachers do that too much. It becomes a habit."

"I guess it would," Mike said. After a small silence he asked, "Do you still take classes to the Badlands?"

"Sure," she said.

"Do they have to go through the nature center?"

"Why? Did you dislike that part?"

"No. But I liked walking around better," Mike said.

"I do, too."

They were quiet, and Mike could hear his mother on the phone, upstairs—the anxious tone of her voice and a few stark words: shock, Glenn, police.

"Donetta and I go out there sometimes," Mike said, to drown out his mother's voice. "We sit on the rocks and watch for mountain goats."

"Do you?"

"I like how empty it is."

"Why?" Noleen asked.

"It's peaceful. It's just you and the rocks."

"And the goats," Noleen said.

"Yeah. And the goats."

They heard something break upstairs, then Mike's

mother saying, "Damn it!" A moment later she came down to the kitchen.

"What was it?" Noleen said. "Let me clean it up."

Carolyn shook her head. She got out a broom and dust-pan and went back upstairs. After that, the light in the kitchen seemed hotter, less bearable. Across from Mike, Noleen moved out of the sun, away from the window.

LATER in the morning, when it was just Mike and his mother at home, a police officer came and asked more questions. But only Tom DeWitt, who arrived at noon, spoke to them at any length. Wearing a shirt and tie, he sat formally with them in the living room. "In a situation like this," he said, "you either find the person by now, or you don't find him for quite a while."

"A situation like this?" Carolyn asked.

"Where the susp—person is intelligent and doesn't have a record."

"You can call him whatever you want," Carolyn said. "We know what he did. We're as horrified by it as you are."

"I'm just saying, don't panic each time the phone rings, or when you see a police car out front. We probably won't have any news for some time."

"I don't know whether that's good or bad," she said, looking at Mike; Mike avoided looking at either of them.

"It's bad for us," the agent said. "I don't know which

would be easier for you." He stood up to leave, then turned to Mike's mother apologetically. "That was insensitive," he told her. "Of course it's hard for you either way."

He opened the front door and closed it silently behind him. From the window, Mike watched him observe the house and yard for a few minutes before getting into his car.

HIS mother spent the early part of the afternoon on the phone; then she and Mike tried to sleep. Mike, in his room, shut the curtains against the sun. In his mind were his mother's conversations with her parents, up in Mobridge—his father's parents were no longer alive—and with insurance people and friends. No one could believe what had happened. No one could have predicted it. No one knew what to say. To Mike it seemed as unreal as it did too real. It was like, only worse, the time Donetta's period didn't come and she did a home pregnancy test that came out positive. Facts were the scariest things there were. Anything else you could change in your head, somehow, make less bad, but a fact was as definite as an object. It stayed where it was until something else happened—in Donetta's case, a miscarriage she'd had three weeks later. Mike took her to the doctor himself; no one else ever knew, and Donetta had never wanted to talk about it again, even to Mike. He remembered what those three weeks were like. And they were nothing compared with this.

He gave up on sleep. He walked past his mother's closed

door and went downstairs to the den. He sat in the armchair his father had sat in to watch television. His father,
who liked mysteries, tried to figure out the endings in advance. "The brother of the priest did it," he'd say to Mike.
"I'll bet you fifty dollars."

"I don't want to bet," Mike would say, meaning, I don't
give a shit who did it and I don't see why you do. But now
it seemed significant, his father caring so much about complicated plots. It revealed something about him. "If you
know enough," Mike's history teacher had said once,
"everything means something." They'd been talking about
wars and how they got started.

It was too hard for Mike to stay in the house. He went
into the backyard and sat on the picnic table they hadn't
used in years. It was stained with birdshit and littered with
twigs. They used to eat out there on summer nights when
Mike was small. The worst thing he ever did to his parents
was grow up. He didn't know where that thought came
from, but he knew it was true. His parents had been happier when they'd had him to take care of.

He went back inside. His mother was still in her room,
and he wrote her a note: "Be back for dinner. Don't worry. I
rode out to the Schofields'."

LEE-ANN came outside as soon as Mike rode up. What
he'd started feeling about her last fall—that he counted on
her for something important—now seemed so true that the

muscles in his legs were quivering, as though he'd ridden his bicycle all the way there instead of his motorcycle.

"Come inside," she told him. "I just made coffee." Neil's white truck wasn't around; Ed's old Corvette was parked near the barn.

Mike took off his helmet and followed her into the kitchen. She was wearing shorts and a T-shirt Mike had given her when he'd outgrown it: WHEATLEY WRESTLING, it said on the back. She used to tease him for wearing it so much. "You just want girls to know you've got muscles," she used to say. From the living room he could hear *The Little Mermaid* playing on the VCR.

"Janna's almost asleep," Lee-Ann said. "Sit down. I didn't think you'd come today."

"I know. I can't stay long."

She poured him coffee with a lot of milk—the only way he could drink it and like the taste. She sat next to him at the table, and when he crossed his legs, jiggling his foot up and down, she reached over and touched his boot. "Don't be nervous," she said.

"Okay. I mean, I'm not, really."

"We kept thinking about you last night," she told him. "We wondered if you were all right, if you could sleep."

He hated that she'd said *we*. Before, he thought, she would have said *I*. "I slept some," Mike said, more conscious than he wanted to be of the shape of her breasts under the white T-shirt. He wasn't ashamed of looking, but he didn't want to be too obvious about it. He made himself look away, at the squares of light on the clean kitchen floor. "My father was having an affair with her," he said then. "Big surprise, right?"

"I guess we all figured that, after what he did."

"I should have known before that," Mike said. "I should have known something was going on."

"Why?" Lee-Ann asked.

Mike looked at her, feeling his face get hot. "You know," he said. "You can tell when there is. People act different around each other."

She hesitated, then said gently, "You've got too much on your mind. You can't think about everything at once. You have too many things happening to you."

Mike felt foolish then, and looked out the window at Route 8 and the distant hills.

"I'm glad you came, though," Lee-Ann said. "I wanted you to know that you could come over and talk. I mean, we're friends. We can talk about things, right?"

"We are talking," Mike said.

"I mean, really talk. Like about how you feel and what's going on in your life. You're not the most talkative person in the world."

"I'm better at other things," Mike said, and as soon as he said it he knew that he'd struck the wrong note.

"That's because those other things are easier," Lee-Ann told him quietly. In the next room *The Little Mermaid* ended, and she went in to see if Janna was asleep. Mike could hear the videotape rewinding, and the ticking of the grandfather clock in the hallway. When she returned, she poured herself more coffee. "Did I make yours too strong?" she asked Mike. He hadn't drunk any.

"No," he said. "I forgot about it."

He watched her remove her barrette, which caused her soft hair to fall against her face. "So did your mother know about your father's affair?" she asked him.

"Not for very long." He told her part of his mother's story, leaving out the fact that she'd asked Mary Hise to stay in her job a few weeks longer. That had become a secret the moment Mike had heard it.

"Why do you think your mother just didn't leave him?" Lee-Ann asked.

"Because she thought it was over."

"But she knew that it had happened."

"I know," Mike said. "Maybe she just didn't care about him enough for it to matter."

"Maybe it was the opposite. Maybe she loved him so much that she was willing to forgive him. Or maybe she just understood how it could happen. Maybe she understood that it would be natural, almost, for people who were around each other a lot." Lee-Ann averted her eyes from Mike's then, and looked down at her coffee.

"For people who were attracted to each other, you mean," Mike said softly. Lee-Ann didn't look at him. "I don't think my mother would understand about that," he said then. "I don't think she loved him a whole lot, either."

"It's hard to tell about a marriage from the outside," Lee-Ann said.

"How outside could I have been?"

But Lee-Ann was watching out the window now, as Neil and Ed came up the long driveway in Neil's white truck. There was a wooden structure in the back of it. "That's an old lean-to they bought," she said. "From somebody out near Red Shirt."

She stood up then, and Mike did, too, and there was a moment before he opened the door when Lee-Ann was close enough for him to smell her clean hair and the lotion on her skin. Neither of them moved. Finally Mike said, "Thanks for the coffee," and let his arm brush against hers as if by accident. Then he walked out into the bright afternoon, keeping himself from turning around to see her again.

NEIL and Ed stopped talking to each other when Mike walked up.

"I'm sorry, Mike," Ed said. "I found out this morning."

"Did you hear it on the news?"

"A neighbor told me. He heard it on the radio."

"Has anything else happened?" Neil asked.

"No. I mean, he hasn't been caught yet." It was a weird thing for Mike to hear himself say. "I mean, found."

The three of them stood there, looking at the old, musty-smelling lean-to. Mike had often heard Neil and Ed say that they would have been happier a hundred years ago, when the West was a frontier—at least more than it was now. But it was hard for Mike to imagine that the past could have given them more than the present did.

"I can't stay long," Mike said to Neil. "But I thought we could fix that fence."

"Screw the fence," Neil said. "Ed and I can do that."

"I hate sitting around," Mike told him. "I'd rather do something."

NEIL and Mike drove out to the farthest pasture, beyond which were pine-covered hills and the late-afternoon sun shining through the tops of the trees. Neil asked how Mike's mother was.

"Tired," Mike said. He told him part of what he had told Lee-Ann. He also told him about the police asking questions, and about how Tom DeWitt wanted to think like Mike's father.

"Good luck," Neil said.

"I know."

They were riding along the fence line, with the windows down, the road less dusty after last night's rain. "I shouldn't have said that," Neil said. "Your father usually seemed all right. But I saw him not too long ago at the bar in Hermosa, giving the waitress a bad time."

"About what?" Mike asked.

"Not coming over to the table enough times, or not talking to him enough—something like that."

"He gets strange sometimes," Mike said, which was such an understatement, given the circumstances, that he stopped talking and looked out the window.

"But then I didn't know him well," Neil said.

He parked on the roadside, and he and Mike got out with their tools. They worked without speaking—Neil faster, as usual, and Mike feeling sluggish, as if he were moving through water. He felt "thick," as Donetta would say, explaining a sensation she had once in a while, lying in bed, when her limbs felt as thick and heavy as logs. "You know why I think that happens?" she'd said to Mike. "Because in my mind I'm trying to fly away from myself, and my body is telling me I can't go. I'm stuck here. Extra gravity is making sure I stay."

"Did my father ever talk about me?" Mike said. He listened to himself say it, conscious of the past tense, and thinking that his voice sounded as fake as it did on the answering machine at home: "The Newlins can't come to the phone right now. Please leave a message, and we'll call you back."

"No," Neil said. "Not that I remember."

They kept working. Mike, kneeling down clumsily, snagged his sleeve on a rusty wire and tried to free it too quickly. He cut his arm pretty badly—more like a rip than a cut.

"Let me see it," Neil said. Mike rolled up his torn sleeve, and Neil went back to the truck for antiseptic and a bandage. "Get a tetanus shot tomorrow," he told Mike.

"I got one last fall," Mike said. "Dad makes me get them more often than I need." He said it without thinking, and suddenly he was trying to keep from crying. He walked away from Neil, toward the wide field beyond Neil's ranch, where at dusk there were almost always ten white-tailed deer. He tried to get control of himself by watching for them now. He didn't know why he was crying. No one had died except somebody he hardly knew. And what his father had done he'd done to her.

"Mike?" Neil said, behind him, not coming closer. He finished the fence himself and waited until Mike walked back toward him before he put the tools in the truck. "Just so you know," he told Mike, "we can help out easily enough, if money's a problem."

"Okay," Mike said. "Thanks."

The sun was setting by then, and as they drove the few miles back to the house Mike fell asleep for a second, dreaming that his father had set fire to the lean-to with somebody inside it. Neil woke him. "It's all right, Mike," he said. "It was just a bad dream."

AT the house, in the kitchen, with Lee-Ann in the next room with Janna, Mike called his mother. "I'm leaving now," he told her. "I didn't mean to stay this late."

Still, he took as long as he could to leave. He drove the tractor into the pole barn and checked on five baby rabbits, born the week before, under the Schofields' porch. Finally he put on his helmet and started his motorcycle. It was twelve miles to the Wheatley water tower, then half a mile more to Mike's house. He'd been riding his motorcycle for two years, but tonight was the first time he'd minded the things he'd heard older riders complain of: bugs, wind shears, cars that followed too closely.

By the time he got home, he was like somebody thirty-five or forty, he thought, who couldn't feel the satisfaction of speed anymore, who just rode a motorcycle to get someplace he didn't want to go.

FIVE

A~T~ nine o'clock on Saturday morning Mike drove to his father's office to unlock the door for an insurance agent named Stuart Wells, from Rapid City. Mike didn't know anything about his father's business, except that it wasn't very profitable.

The office was on Collier Street and shared a building and parking lot with Anderson Chiropractic Arts. Mike arrived before the insurance agent did and sat in his mother's Buick to wait; his father's car had been impounded by the police. Mike watched people walk into the laundromat across the street.

It was a sunny, warm morning, gusts of wind whipping up dirt from a construction site half a block away, where a new police station was being built to replace the deteriorating building behind the public library. Fewer than four thousand people lived in Wheatley. Mike had lived there all his life. He recognized two of the people driving past, both slowing down when they saw his mother's car, then him. Neither stopped, but both of them—classmates from high school—honked and waved. Mike hadn't ridden his motorcycle because he would have felt that much more conspicuous. He was still conspicuous, but it was better than going inside. He turned the ignition key and listened to the only cassette his mother had that wasn't classical— Keith Whitley. Mike had given it her.

Stuart Wells drove up in a new Chevy. "I thought your mother was supposed to be here," he said when Mike got out of the car. He was a heavy man, younger than Mike's father, with slicked-back, wet-looking hair.

"She didn't feel well," Mike told him. "She asked me to do it." He unlocked the door but didn't go in himself. The insurance agency was a wide room partitioned into two sections—a larger space on the left, for Mike's father, and a smaller space on the right for the receptionist. The spaces were open in front, then separated farther back by a thin, laminated wall. Through the window Mike watched Stuart Wells go straight to his father's computer.

Less than a minute later Tom DeWitt showed up. He had on jeans and cowboy boots—dressed as if he could have been anyone, Mike thought. "I'm glad you're here," he said to Mike. "I wanted to look around a little."

"I thought you came yesterday."

"I wanted to see it again." He put his hand on Mike's

back at the same time that he opened the door to walk inside, so that Mike had no choice but to go in with him. He introduced himself to Stuart Wells. "You're getting his accounts?" he asked.

"The few he had."

"It's a shame it's not quality that matters in business," Tom DeWitt said lightly, and moved into the other part of the office, where Mike was standing.

"My father wanted to be an engineer," Mike said. "It was only when that didn't work out that he settled for insurance."

"Is that right?"

"Yes, sir."

Mike watched him turn on Mary Hise's computer, look through the papers on her desk, and empty out a white plastic container, shaped like a lamb, that held pens and pencils. "Call me Tom," he said to Mike. "I don't like *sir.*"

"It's what I was brought up to say."

"Did your father make you call him sir?"

"No," Mike said. "He didn't make me do anything."

Tom sat in Mary Hise's chair—a cushioned brown office chair that swiveled and could be adjusted up or down. He looked through her desk drawers and filing cabinets. In the back of one drawer, under office stationery, he found the photograph of Mary and her dog that she had shown Mike that day in December. "She had a dog?" Tom said. He stood up, holding the photograph. "Where is it, then?"

"I don't know," Mike said.

"But it was hers."

"I guess."

Tom took the photograph and went outside, motioning for Mike to walk out with him. They stood between their cars. "Do you know anything at all about Mary Hise?" he said.

"Not really."

"Her parents are on a camping trip in Canada. We can't get in touch with them. We've reached a brother in Sioux Falls, who hasn't seen his sister in two years. He wants us to keep the body here until his parents get back." Tom put on his sunglasses. "Does that seem cold to you?"

"I don't know," Mike said. "I hardly knew her."

"Would you like to see where she lived?"

"No," Mike said. "Why would I?" Then he realized how unfeeling that sounded. "Why do you want me to?"

"I thought you might be curious. I'm going there now, anyway." He opened the passenger door of his car. "Get in. I'll give you a ride back here afterward." Mike hesitated, and Tom said, "You don't have to come if it makes you uneasy."

"It doesn't make me uneasy."

"Good," Tom said. "Get in."

They drove past the construction site and the elementary school, and past Saint Ann's, the small Episcopal church Mike's mother attended weekly and Mike attended on Christmas and Easter. His father used to belong to the Lutheran church his parents had attended—they were

buried in the cemetery beside it—but Mike couldn't remember his father ever having gone to a service. "I don't
believe there's a God," he'd told Mike recently, one Sunday
morning. "Not many people are brave enough to say that."

Behind the trailer park on Montana Street, Tom DeWitt
parked in front of an older two-story building divided into
apartments. Mary Hise's was on the first floor, second from
the end. There was a cement walkway that ran the length
of the building.

"You shouldn't be here," he told Mike, unlocking the
door. "So don't mention it to anyone."

"I can wait outside."

"No. Go ahead and look around." He took off his sunglasses and turned on the kitchen light. "Just walk
through the rooms," he said. He stayed behind, in the
kitchen.

It was eerie for Mike to be there. He looked at the walls,
which were in need of paint, and the green carpeting covering the uneven floors. She hadn't had much furniture, just
the basic things, like a couch and coffee table, a television
but not a VCR. Mike walked into each room, knowing
that what Tom DeWitt wanted was for him to feel worse
than he did about Mary Hise's death. And he did think he
should feel sorrier. But no one had forced Mary Hise to be
with his father.

He stood longest in her bedroom, looking at the radio
and lamp on her nightstand and at the yellow curtains on
the small window. On top of her bureau he read what was

on a slip of paper: "milk," "tomato soup," and "frozen peas." Next to it was a framed picture of herself—her high school graduation picture, Mike guessed, because she looked younger, her smile hesitant or uncertain.

On her double bed was a thick, yellow-flowered comforter. Mike wondered how many times his father had been in that bed with her. It was even more disturbing for him to imagine her in it alone, because he could still envision how she'd looked in a bathing suit. Behind the door— Mike almost didn't see it—was a laundry hamper with pink underwear thrown on top.

In her bathroom he looked at her toothbrush and toothpaste, her comb and brush, and something Mike knew his father had given her: a little porcelain hummingbird on a green base. It used to be in the upstairs bathroom of Mike's house, until his mother had said, "Let's get rid of that thing." She'd forgotten that it had belonged to Mike's grandmother—Glenn's mother—and Mike's father hadn't reminded her.

Mike went back into the kitchen, where Tom DeWitt pointed out to him a bowl of water on the floor. "It was under the edge of the dishwasher," he told Mike. "We missed it somehow."

He had opened all the cabinets; in the back of the second one were three cans of dog food. "How does your father feel about dogs?" he asked Mike, before picking up the phone and dialing. Mike didn't answer. He was looking at the magnets on her refrigerator door, each one a miniature kitchen gadget. Under the teakettle was a reminder of a dental appointment on June 22, two days from then. Mike was thinking that Mary Hise had been only six years older than he was, and that she'd talked to him that day in December as if she might be lonely.

Behind him, on the phone, he heard Tom DeWitt say, "This is our fuck-up. We should have known Thursday."

TOM drove back to the insurance agency by way of the root-beer stand on Laramie Street. "Do you mind?" he asked Mike. "I'm thirsty." He got a root beer for each of them, and they drank them in the car. Across the street was the post office, a square stone building designed a long time ago by somebody famous, whose name Mike couldn't remember. Mike watched as somebody from out of town— Oregon, her license plate read—snapped a picture of it.

Tom turned toward Mike. "Do you know how Mary ended up in Wheatley?" he asked. "She moved here a year and a half ago, to be close to a boyfriend working on that dude ranch south of town. We learned that from a neighbor."

Mike didn't say anything. He didn't want to seem interested.

"According to the neighbor, the boyfriend moved away last October, then came back for a visit. We're trying to find him. Do you know anything about him?"

"No."

Tom looked at Mike in a friendly way. "Did you open Mary's closets or drawers?"

"Of course not."

"Well, you should have, because they're interesting. My sister's a buyer for a department store in Rapid City. I brought her over here last night to look at Mary's clothes. I said, 'Tell me what kind of person she was.'" He put his empty glass down on the seat. "I don't know anything about women's clothes. And neither do the female agents I know. Not like my sister does. It's a specialty, like anything else. To be a good detective, you have to be smart enough to know who the experts are." He smiled at Mike. "That's my ego talking. So now you know I think I'm smart."

"Why do you care about her clothes?"

"I don't, exactly. But you can never predict what things will be important and what things won't."

He took Mike's empty glass from him, picked up his own, and returned them to the person behind the counter. He had an easy walk that Mike didn't trust. He'd seen wrestlers who walked that way, who could move as if they were less muscular than they were. They were so flexible that their strength was disguised, and they fooled you into thinking they couldn't take control.

Tom got back in and put on his seat belt. "What was I saying?" he asked Mike.

"You were talking about your sister."

He pulled back onto Laramie. "She looked through the

closet and dresser and said that Mary probably hadn't bought much since high school. My sister dated the clothes. Just like a coroner figuring out when somebody died."

He drove past Wheatley Western Wear and the Rush School of Beauty, which Donetta's mother owned, and stopped at the red light on the corner of Pearson Street. "My sister said that Mary bought childish-looking clothes," he told Mike. "Things that hid her body, especially her breasts. Mary wanted to look younger, and maybe more carefree than she was. She didn't want to be held responsible. And something major must have happened to her in high school, my sister said, to make her quit shopping. I laughed when she said that, but she was serious. For girls, my sister told me, not shopping anymore is like not sleeping, or not eating. It's a sign of disturbance."

They were back at the insurance agency. Tom pulled in next to Mike's mother's Buick. "What do you think?" he asked Mike, as if they'd been exchanging opinions all along, as if he hadn't done all the talking.

"I don't see why Mary Hise matters so much. It's not her you're trying to find."

"Do you think it's random," Tom DeWitt said, "who people end up with? Don't you think you can define people by who they choose? For example, what kind of wife do you think I'd have?"

"Mary Hise wasn't married to him."

"Sometimes wives and lovers are the same people, and sometimes they're not."

Mike looked at his mother's dark red car. "If a person has a wife and a girlfriend," he said carefully, "which one do you define the person by?"

"Which do you think?"

"I have no idea."

"Well, you get a third defining thing," Tom said, "which is the fact of the girlfriend—the fact that he'd have one."

"So I guess you think that automatically makes somebody a bad person," Mike said. "Like you and people like you are in a special category. You're always faithful, and you're never for one minute attracted to somebody else."

"I don't know," Tom said. "I've never been married."

"But I'm supposed to guess what your wife is like?" Mike opened the car door angrily. "You try to trick people you think aren't as smart as you. You think you know people when you don't know shit about them." He banged his knee on the dashboard as he got out, and shut the door as hard as he could. He was so unnerved that he tried to open his mother's car with the wrong key.

Finally, leaving the parking lot and driving home, he said to the empty car, "Her dog's name is Harrison. And my father would sooner shoot a person than a dog."

He didn't see the humor of it until after he'd said it, and then he understood for the first time something his English teacher had once said, quoting some dead writer: "Humor is almost never about happiness."

SIX

THE fact that Mike knew these small things became more important to him than the things themselves. They wouldn't have given Tom DeWitt much more information than he had figured out on his own. But they made Mike feel more in control. He found himself repeating them in his mind, along with something else that only he and his mother knew: that when Mike was in the fourth grade, and their dog, Lucky, had been killed by a car, Mike's father had been so grief-stricken that he'd walked around the house half the night and had never allowed them to get another pet. His father's reaction had seemed extreme even to Mike, who had loved the dog as much as anyone did. Even more extreme was that a month later, when Mike's parents had driven Mike to summer camp, his father had seemed unable to leave him there. Mike remembered standing in a clearing with his duffel bag, watching his mother help his weeping father into the passenger seat, so that she could drive him home.

Mike didn't tell anyone about going to Mary Hise's apartment. He would have felt like a traitor, not to his father but to his mother. What made him angry was knowing that Tom DeWitt probably counted on that; he and Mike had a secret now. And it was hard for Mike to stop thinking about that apartment, especially about Mary Hise's pink underwear on top of the hamper. It wasn't a perverted thing that he felt, though. It was just too private, and he pictured her in it even though he didn't want to.

HE spent that Saturday afternoon and the rest of the weekend mowing the yard, trimming hedges, and cleaning out the gutters. He didn't know what else to do. He would have worked at the ranch, but his mother had said that they should both stay home. She said that on Monday they would go back to work and try to get back into a regular routine.

They had their meals in the kitchen instead of the dining room; the dining room table was covered with documents his mother was going through—bank statements, insurance policies, and the mortgage information on the house. "We have to act as if he's never coming back," she told Mike. Sometimes she got emotional, but other times she got angry. She snapped at him about tracking grass clippings into the kitchen; she insisted that he come in and eat the second she wanted him to.

On Sunday morning Mike was relieved to see Noleen Watkins come over to have breakfast with them and to attend church with his mother. As they were eating, Noleen listed all the people who had asked about Carolyn and Mike. "Everyone's sympathetic," she said. "People are concerned about you two." Mike's mother had been afraid that she might have trouble at work, but her principal and vice principal had called, asking what they could do to help. Only a few people had called in order to fish for details.

And the phone was tapped. The Division of Criminal Investigation had gotten permission to do it, although even Tom DeWitt had told them to stop thinking that the next call might be from Glenn. Mike didn't think his father would call, anyway. He'd let more time pass, if he called at all. "How could he face talking to us?" Mike's mother said now, to Noleen. But Mike thought of it differently. He thought that his father might be not ready yet to tell them what really happened, why he did what he did. There might be some reason that he couldn't explain yet.

Mike waited for his mother and Noleen to leave for church before calling Josh Mitchell, in Sheridan, Wyoming. He'd been waiting to be alone to do it. Mike and Josh had been best friends almost all of their lives, and Mike hadn't seen him since February, when Josh had moved away. When school was in session they'd E-mailed each other—whatever they could get away with in case their teachers were reading the mail. Josh would quote from a book he'd made up, called *Sexual Guide for Teenagers in the Twenty-first Century.* He'd quote things like, "Girls: Keep in mind that oral sex is a healthy alternative to intercourse."

"I heard about your dad on the news," Josh said now, when Mike called. "I didn't know what the fuck to do. My dad said, 'Let him call you first, when he's ready.' But, then, my dad's a prick."

Mike couldn't let himself laugh.

"Your mom must be freaking out," Josh said. He cleared his throat. He was doing something in the background—making coffee, Mike guessed. Josh had started drinking coffee when he was twelve. "I like the buzz," he used to tell Mike.

"She's at church right now," Mike said. "Ms. Watkins went with her."

"Is Watkins still fucking Coach?" Josh asked. "Wait," he said then. "I'm being an asshole." He was quiet for a moment. Then he spoke in a more serious voice. "It seems crazy. How could he do that? That's what I said when I heard it on the news. My dad said, 'People can do anything.'"

"I know some stuff," Mike said awkwardly. "He was, you know, seeing her." He didn't feel like saying "fucking," or even "sleeping with."

"I figured that," Josh said. He was quiet again. Mike

knew that Josh's mother had had an affair; that was why his parents had split up. Josh had told Mike later who it was—Duane King, who owned King Trucking Company. She was still with him.

"Anyway," Mike said, "we're being listened to. The police are tapping the phone in case he calls."

"Which he won't."

"I don't think so, either."

"Well, shit," Josh said. "Now I feel like saying more about Watkins and Coach."

Mike laughed. It felt good, but unfamiliar, to do it.

AT four o'clock that afternoon, as Mike was wishing he could find an excuse to see Lee-Ann Schofield, or to call her at least, Tom DeWitt came over again. He said that the district attorney would try to go before a grand jury to get an indictment. "You can bypass a preliminary hearing if there's enough evidence," he said.

Mike didn't really know what that meant. The three of them stood in the stuffy living room, his mother not responding either. Earlier, when she'd come home from church, she'd just sat on her bed for almost an hour. Mike had gone upstairs twice and walked past her open door; he'd been afraid to ask if she was all right for fear that she wasn't. Finally, he'd just stood in the hallway between her room and his. He'd told himself that he really wasn't all that frightened. But when she came out of her room he found that his back hurt from standing so rigidly.

Now, in their living room, Tom DeWitt said, "There's the gun with Glenn's fingerprints on it. In addition, the clerk at the motel identified him from a photograph. There are the money transfers, his fingerprints on the phone, and so on." He sat down on the couch without being invited to. "I wouldn't typically tell the suspect's family any of this."

"We want to know," Carolyn said. "Glenn should have to pay for what he did." She turned to Mike for confirmation, but he kept his eye on the window behind her.

"Not all families would feel that way," Tom said.

No one spoke. After a moment Carolyn politely asked, "Would you like coffee?"

"I would," he said. "Thanks." After she left the room he unbuttoned and rolled up his shirtsleeves. The day had been dry and hot; the temperature had reached a hundred. The windows were open, but there was almost no breeze. "Your mom's a nice person," Tom told Mike.

"What do you think is nice about her?"

"She has dignity."

Mike looked out the window at Mr. Hyler, across the street, watering the geraniums on his front porch. "She always does what she's supposed to," he said. "That's not hard to do."

"Some people find it impossible." On Tom's face was

that pleasant expression Mike didn't trust. He seemed re-laxed, as if their house had become a familiar place to him.

Mike waited impatiently for his mother to come back in. She shouldn't have left him alone with Tom DeWitt. How did she think he'd feel, sitting there? He concentrated on Lee-Ann and how her breasts had felt against him that Saturday afternoon in the barn, when he'd held her, finally. He needed more moments like that with her. They gave him a way to feel sexual that nobody else knew about. They made the life inside his head count for more than the life outside it.

When his mother did come in, bringing coffee, she and Tom DeWitt talked about ordinary things—about Tom's brother, who taught at the elementary school, and about Tom's nephew, Kyle, who'd wrestled with Mike. In the fall Kyle was going to attend Black Hills State University, in Spearfish. "It's the only place he got accepted," Tom said.

"Maybe he just applied too late," Mike said.

"No. He didn't get the grades you did."

"How do you know what grades I got?"

"Mike," his mother said warningly.

"Kyle told me. He was envious of you, I think."

"Not anymore, probably."

Mike ignored the look his mother gave him and went upstairs to his room. He couldn't stand that his mother and Tom DeWitt were talking as if they'd become friends. Mike's mother was liable to say anything. Like what, he thought then. What did she know? Whose side was she on? That was stupid, he knew. Taking sides was what you did in junior high school, when your friends got pissed-off at each other and you had to make a choice.

He sat at his desk, then stood restlessly in front of the window. After he saw Tom leave, he went downstairs and outside, changed the oil in his motorcycle, and rode around the block. He thought about riding out to the Schofields', then realized that he'd forgotten his helmet. That was something his mother got furious with him about. His father did too, but his father had been unpredictable—like if Mike had driven the car and left it only a quarter full of gas, sometimes his father had gotten mad and sometimes he hadn't. Sometimes he'd even laughed—as if, since he was in a good mood, what difference did it make what Mike did? But it worked the other way, too. There'd never been a way to change his father's mood from bad to good.

Mike, depressed now, put his motorcycle in the carport. He sat in the backyard and looked at the oak tree in the Pates' yard, next door. He remembered the times he'd climbed it—falling, once, fifteen feet, and how even though he'd been all right his father had taken him to the emergency room and woken him up several times that night, to make sure that he wasn't unconscious. It was painful for Mike to think about that. It was easier to think of his father as a bad or fucked-up person.

His mother came to the kitchen door. "Why didn't you wear your helmet?" she asked.

"I forgot it. So I came back."

Reluctantly, he sat with her in the kitchen while she cooked, and they ate without mentioning his father or Tom DeWitt. His mother didn't eat much, not that she'd ever eaten all that much. She was thin by nature, but also she didn't overdo anything. She didn't drink, she never went over the speed limit, and she didn't spend too much money. It seemed to Mike that she turned not overdoing things into a fault.

What she talked about now was that financially they'd be all right. The money they'd saved for his college tuition was safe; his father hadn't touched that. At some point Mike might have to work part-time, but didn't a lot of students work these days? She talked as if his father and whatever happened to him was irrelevant.

Outside, a sparrow perched on the clothesline and a squirrel ran past the shed. The light was gentler, almost golden, and across the grass were long evening shadows.

"What do you think will happen?" Mike said, and felt odd, asking that. He wasn't used to talking to his mother as if they were allies—on the same side of things.

"I don't know. I can't even guess. I didn't know him, apparently."

She carried their plates to the sink. Mike usually washed the dinner dishes—the house had been built before dishwashers were installed, and they'd never bought one—but his mother was already doing them. The kitchen was large and square, with yellow linoleum and white curtains. It was homey, his mother always said. Her parents—Mike's grandparents, who lived upstate in Mobridge—had a house that wasn't homey. It was as upright as they were. They had wanted to come to Wheatley when Mike's mother had told them what happened, but his mother had said no, thank you for offering. To Mike she had said, "As if I could stand for them to see me like this." She was an only child, just as he was.

Mike wiped off the table and told his mother that he didn't want dessert; maybe he'd have pie at Andell's Diner. He was going there to meet Donetta. He would have gone even if his mother had asked him not to. But Noleen Watkins and another teacher were coming over, to keep his mother company, and he left her standing in the kitchen, making sure that he remembered his helmet.

IN the fading light, Mike rode his motorcycle through town and out on the highway to the diner that had been there since before he was born. He sat alone at a back booth, waiting for Donetta to finish her shift. He drank a Coke and ate a piece of cherry pie. It was painful for him to sit there, even though the diner was half empty and he didn't recognize anyone. In fact he thought it might be easier if he did know people; then they'd at least have to keep quiet or treat him the way Mr. Andell had when Mike first walked in—as if Mike had knives stuck in him and Mr. Andell were afraid to mention them or pull them out. As it was, though, Mike overheard a man say, "What I don't understand is why, if he was trying to kill her, the son of a bitch called an ambulance."

Donetta's shift was over at eight. Mike left his motorcycle in the parking lot, and they took her Geo out to Crow Lake, the violet sky in front of them darkening. Mike drove, and once they were on the two-lane county road she changed clothes, taking off her dirty uniform and her underwear, and putting on a pair of cutoff jeans and a tank top.

Mike was almost used to seeing Donetta naked. She was the second girl he had slept with—when he was in the tenth grade and she was in the ninth. Over the past three years they'd broken up twice, seen other people, and come back together. They became a more permanent couple after Donetta's father died, when she was fifteen and a half. Her parents had gotten divorced six years earlier; her father, the manager of a hardware store, had lived in Hot Springs with a woman who was an alcoholic.

"He took care of her," Donetta had explained to Mike. Her father had died suddenly, of a heart attack, and Donetta had said that his heart had always been a problem; he'd always had too many emotions.

Crow Lake was six miles southwest of Wheatley, a large manmade lake on land that once had been a family-owned ranch; now it was owned by the government. There were cottonwood trees along the western edge and an outcropping of limestone on the southern side. To the north and east were fields of prairie grass long enough to disappear in.

Mike parked the Geo under the trees, and he and Donetta spread a blanket next to the water. They were the only people there, on that side; across the lake some teenagers were swimming. They could just barely see them. High school kids often swam there. Every once in a while, maybe once every three or four years, somebody drank too much and drowned.

"I had a sex dream about us last night," Donetta said. "I woke up thinking, you don't know where your father is, or if you'll ever see him again, and all that's on my mind is fucking you."

She lay back on the blanket and pulled up her tank top so that Mike could see her smooth, tan stomach—her mother's beauty school had a tanning booth. "Tell me if I'm getting fat," she said. "I eat french fries at work, and sometimes coconut cream pie."

"You're nowhere near fat," Mike told her.

"Well, I've been running farther," Donetta said. "I wanted to surprise you when I got up to six miles, and it happened this morning. I ran out of town all the way to Lame Johnny Creek, to that tree that leans down over the water."

"You shouldn't run alone that far out of Wheatley," Mike said. "Most people who use that road don't even live around here."

Donetta opened her mouth to speak, then didn't. She put her hand on Mike's hair. "You know what I almost said? That strangers are probably not more dangerous than people you know. I feel like I can't say anything anymore without having it mean too many things."

They lay close to each other and watched the stars appear, with the Milky Way just above them, and no moon. They heard the teenagers drive away.

"I don't care about your father, or what he did," Donetta whispered. "I really don't. I just care about us." She sat up halfway, leaned over Mike, and unbuttoned his shirt. Her long hair was loose, and the ends of it brushed across his neck and chest. She undid his belt and unzipped his jeans. "What do you think?" she said softly. "Don't you think this will feel good?"

He closed his eyes and put his hands on her hair, then under her tank top and under the waistband of her shorts. She didn't wear underwear any more than she had to; she'd said that once to Mike's mother. It was true that she liked to shock people, but at the same time she was honest and almost naïve. For example, she couldn't believe that his mother had later said to him, "A girl like that has no intention of being faithful to anyone."

"What does that have to do with underwear?" Donetta had said. And she was right, because she was completely and sometimes ridiculously loyal. She'd once gone around for months with frizzy, orange hair—and not the stylish kind—because her sister, Margo, had colored and permed it.

She was ten times more faithful than Mike was. Now, for

example, with his hands on her hair and skin, he was thinking about Lee-Ann Schofield. And before he'd become so attracted to Lee-Ann, he'd thought of a dark-haired girl who sat in front of him in eleventh-grade homeroom. It was almost second nature to him, to be thinking of another girl when he was with Donetta, and to sometimes think of Donetta when he was with someone else. He did it so automatically that he didn't question or judge it, but he knew that it influenced what he thought about himself.

"I'm good at being analytical and objective," he wrote in his college application essay. "I think that, more than most people, I'm capable of standing outside a situation. One thing I could improve on, though, is knowing when it might help to do the opposite, and take more part in things."

"What did you mean by that?" his mother had asked him when she proofread it. "I don't know," he'd said. "It was just what I was thinking."

"Did you bring condoms?" Donetta whispered to him. She was sitting up now, taking off her shorts and tank top. It was too dark to see anything except the stars reflected on the water and, up close, Donetta's tan skin, pale in the darkness.

He had sex with her. She called it either fucking or making love, depending on the mood she was in; to him it was a more generic thing. But tonight Mary Hise—the way she would have looked naked—came into his mind for just a

second and scared Mike so much that he not only concentrated on Donetta, he even said, "I love you" when he had
an orgasm. He didn't usually say that to her unless she said
it to him first, and that was what made her cry.

"I love you, too," she said. "But you know I do. It's not
like I keep it a secret."

She turned away from him and put on her clothes. He
dressed, too, and they got in her car and sat with the windows down, listening to the frogs.

"Don't think you shouldn't use that word again,"
Donetta said. "My father used to tell me, 'Tears are just salt
water.' "

She moved close to Mike, and he kept one arm around
her as they drove back to Andell's Diner, where Mike got
his motorcycle and followed Donetta to her house. Mrs.
Rush had a rule: If Donetta was out with a boy, she needed
to be brought home by that boy. "That's civilized behavior," Mrs. Rush had told Mike a long time ago. "The boy
comes in and says a proper good night and thank you.
That's how I should have been raised."

The lights were on at Donetta's house. She lived half a
mile east of Wheatley on Flat Rock Road, at the edge of a
small crop of new houses. Her house had been the first one
built out there. It was a one-story aluminum-sided home
with an attached garage. It looked more expensive than it
was. Inside, the walls were not nearly as thick as they were
in Mike's house. But there were nice, modern things about

it, like a built-in microwave and a bathtub you could turn into a Jacuzzi.

Donetta lived there with her mother, her twenty-eight-year-old sister, Margo, and Margo's sometimes husband, Cory Burris—sometimes because he came and went as he pleased, driving up to Montana on the spur of the moment, or riding his Harley into Sturgis in August, for the Black Hills Biker Rally, and not coming back until September. He worked occasionally as a trucker; mainly it was Margo who supported them, working with her mother at the beauty school in Wheatley and helping her open a second one in Rapid City.

Cory Burris was a weight lifter; he was big and tough-looking but quiet-spoken. He drove Mrs. Rush crazy. Donetta's favorite story was the night her mother had drunk too much and gone after Cory with the B–C volume of the encyclopedia. "Just don't make me read it," Cory had said. Lately, Mrs. Rush, Cory, and Margo had been seeing a Christian therapist in Rapid City.

Tonight they were all in the kitchen, waiting for a pan of brownies to be done. They were sitting at the blue Formica table at the far end of the room, under the dormer window. This was the first time Mike had been over since his father's crime, and he stood self-consciously in the doorway. They were all looking at him.

"Mike!" Mrs. Rush said. "Come and sit down. Get him a chair, Cory."

"I can't stay," Mike told her. "I just wanted to bring Donetta home."

"Just stay for a brownie," Margo said. "We've got five minutes left on the timer."

Cory was bringing in a chair from the dining room, and Mike took it from him and sat down. Donetta sat beside him. Donetta didn't look like her mother or her sister— they were both bigger-boned and bigger-hipped, with dark hair and eyes. Donetta took after her father, who had been slight, with light-brown hair and blue eyes. Mike had seen pictures of him. Donetta's father had had the same interested expression Donetta often had—as if he'd had more questions about life, or himself, than most people had.

"How's your bike running?" Cory asked Mike.

"Okay. A little rough, still."

"I'll take a look at her next time you come over."

"Is your mother all right?" Mrs. Rush said. "I wasn't sure if I should call or not. I knew her teacher friends would be calling."

"She's okay," Mike said. "I'll tell her you asked about her."

Mrs. Rush was wearing a long pink housecoat that zipped up the front. She had unpinned her hair, which was shoulder-length and wavy; now, down around her face, it made her look older but more attractive, Mike thought— like a reminder that even women older than his mother still had sex, though as far as Mike knew, Mrs. Rush wasn't having any these days. "Will you tell me if there's anything

I can do?" she asked Mike. "That way I can help without bothering her."

"Yes, ma'am," Mike said.

The timer went off, and Margo rose to get the brownies out of the oven. She had on a short, silky robe that brushed Mike's arm as she walked past.

"Mrs. Newlin is teaching at the community college this summer," Donetta told her mother.

"I admire someone that educated," Mrs. Rush said to Mike. "A lot of people take that for granted, but I don't."

"High school was enough for me," Cory said.

"Is that why you couldn't be bothered to finish?" Mrs. Rush asked.

"That's a past-history question," Margo told her mother. "Pastor Kelly said we can only talk about things that happen now."

"It would help if certain people were actually doing something now," Mrs. Rush said.

There was a moment of silence. Cory looked at Mike, then up at the ceiling, and Donetta's cat, Sophie, appeared from the hallway and jumped up on Margo's lap.

"Maybe Cory and I can't live here under these circumstances," Margo said. "Maybe we can't even stay here in the same town."

"All I did was ask a question," Mrs. Rush said. "Don't make a federal case out of it."

Donetta took Mike's hand. "Do you want a brownie?" she asked him gently.

Mrs. Rush looked at him. "My goodness," she said. "Take all you want. Wrap them up and take them with you. They'll only make us fatter."

"No, thanks," Mike said. "But I should get going."

He carried his chair back to the dining room, said good night, and walked outside with Donetta. They stood in the driveway and looked at the sprinkling of lights in the houses behind them. "Mom doesn't think about what she says," Donetta told him. "That 'federal case' thing was just an accident."

"I know."

Donetta put her arms around Mike. "You're the only good part of my life," she whispered. "You're the only happy thing I have."

He held her. Across Flat Rock Road was a field that in the darkness looked like water, except that it didn't reflect the stars.

"Me, too," Mike said. He put on his helmet, got on his motorcycle, and rode down the driveway toward Wheatley, and home.

SEVEN

M IKE and his mother went back to work on Monday, though nothing about their lives felt the same. To Mike it was as if they'd woken up in a different house, in another town—almost as if they'd woken up as different people. They were both moodier now, and when Mike heard his mother crying late Monday night, in her room, he didn't know what to do. He felt too awkward and unsettled by it to go in and talk to her; instead, he turned on the radio and listened through his headphones to the all-night rock-and-roll station from Rapid City. He listened to the disc jockey announce who was sending what love song out to whom.

Mike didn't eat breakfast with the Schofields anymore—he felt too guilty now that his mother was alone. She got up early and made him scrambled eggs or waffles, neither of which she would eat. She'd have only cereal or toast, then come outside with her coffee as he got his motorcycle out of the carport.

"Make sure you drink enough water on these hot days," she'd tell him; she didn't seem to want him to leave. She wasn't anxious to go to work herself. "People at the college are being kind," she told Mike one night at supper. "But that just makes me more uncomfortable."

Mike knew what she meant. Neil went out of his way to be nice to him. He paid Mike more per hour than he had been, and when Mike objected Neil said, "We can afford it. And we were underpaying you before." That second part wasn't true.

Ed gave Mike a present for his mother, a large yellow bowl he'd made, which Mike knew would sell for something like sixty or seventy dollars.

The hardest thing for Mike—the change in his life that felt the worst—was that Lee-Ann was never sexy with him anymore. She was friendly and kind, the way that Neil was, and she avoided being alone with him. The only time he saw even a hint of who she used to be with him was one morning when he was working outside the barn without his shirt on. She walked past, holding Janna, and when he caught her watching him she seemed embarrassed to have been caught.

The only people at the ranch who treated him normally were Janna, of course, and Arthur Strong and Louis Ivy. Mike wasn't sure if they knew about his father—although it seemed unlikely that they didn't. "I'm not sure they know your last name," Neil had said to Mike. But Neil underestimated people, the same way he underestimated the importance of money to people who didn't have much. Lately Mike had noticed more negative things about Neil than he had before. He found himself thinking words like "spoiled" and "egotistical"—words Mike's father had used that Mike had objected to. Then he felt guilty. Neil had always been a friend to him, whereas what kind of friend was Mike when it came to the way he felt about Lee-Ann? He'd hate himself for a moment, after which he'd think, I'm only eighteen. She doesn't take me seriously. And we really haven't done anything.

All the time, though, every day since June 18, these thoughts and others were dwarfed by fears about his father: where he might be and what might happen to him. One evening, riding home from the Schofields', he almost ran into a pickup that braked in front of him. His reactions weren't quick anymore. He wasn't focused on what was happening. He was always preoccupied.

ON Friday a rainstorm blew up, and Mike came home from the Schofields' early. He sat in his room, looking through his college brochures at pictures of the campus and of the dorm where he would be living. He had a letter saying who his roommate would be and what his interests were: Raymond Nelson, an honors student from Aberdeen. A computer nerd, he sounded like to Mike. But college seemed too far in the future, and unrealistically carefree. College was where people went before their real lives began, Mike thought; his own life had gotten an early start on real.

From downstairs now, he could hear NPR on the radio, and he went down to the kitchen and cut up potatoes as his mother made pork chops. In her dark skirt and blouse, her short hair combed back from her face, she looked to him like a spinsterish school teacher.

"Slice them thinner," she told Mike, and then, "Would you set the table, please?" It was a relief when the phone rang, until Mike, listening to his mother talk, knew that it was Tom DeWitt. He was calling with the first news about Mike's father: Mary Hise's car, an older-model Chevy Cavalier, had been found in the parking lot of an all-night supermarket in Salt Lake City. Tom DeWitt asked if he could stop over after supper, to talk in person.

THEY had just finished eating when Tom came, too early, and to the kitchen door instead of the front door—as if he wanted to be thought of as a friend, Mike thought, somebody who thought about their interests instead of his own. He stood in the kitchen in a wet windbreaker, saying, "I wonder why Glenn chose Salt Lake City. Why not Denver or Omaha?" He spoke as if he were talking to himself, Mike saw; he was watching for their reactions while pretending not to.

"Isn't that where Dad's friend lives?" Mike said to his

mother. "Didn't Dad say he'd hide Dad if he ever killed anybody?"

His mother stared at him.

"I guess that means you don't know," Tom said.

"Nothing about this is funny," Carolyn said to Mike, and he noticed how quickly she moved their plates out of the way and how politely she asked Tom to sit down. Tom was removing his windbreaker already and putting it over the back of the chair. Under it he had on workout clothes—nylon pants and a stretched-out T-shirt too small for him. He was a gym rat, Mike realized, which was Josh's name for guys they saw in gyms who seemed either shy or dangerous, not usually anything in between.

"We don't know anyone in Salt Lake City," Carolyn told Tom. "We have some friends here, of course. But we're not very social people." She stood at the screen door and looked outside. The sky was gray with rain. "What else have you learned?" she asked. "What was found inside the car?"

"A dress in a dry cleaner's bag" was all Tom DeWitt listed. There must have been more in the car than that, Mike thought. "A short dress," Tom told them. "Denim, I think it was. I can't figure out why Glenn didn't get rid of it. I don't suppose it has any significance for either of you."

"No," Carolyn said.

Mike shook his head, although he was almost sure that that day in December, when they'd talked, Mary Hise had been wearing that dress. He remembered because of the way she'd buttoned and unbuttoned the top two buttons as he was standing there—it was sexy, the way she hadn't seemed to know she was doing it. But he wasn't about to say that he remembered it. That would make him guilty of paying Mary Hise too much attention.

"Why should we know anything about her dress?" Carolyn asked.

"No reason. I just thought I'd ask." Tom crossed his legs and turned to Mike. "Girls and their dresses," he said. "It's a mystery to us, isn't it? Why they put on one and not another."

I thought she wasn't wearing any, Mike almost said.

It was thundering outside, and rain was pouring out of the gutters and pounding the concrete patio outside the screen door. Mike's mother was sitting up very straight, very stiffly. "Mary Hise's parents must know by now," she said. "Do you know when the funeral was?" she asked Tom.

"Three days ago."

"I didn't have the courage to ask. I don't suppose there's anything I could do, by way of apology."

"Apology for what?" Tom said. "What did you do?"

She hesitated. "You know what I did," she said. "I told Mary not to quit yet. I told her to give Glenn some time to get used to . . ." She didn't finish. She got up, filled the sink with soapy water, and stood at the counter with her back to them. She didn't seem able to speak.

Mike stood up quickly and said, "I'll do the dishes, Mom. Go in the other room if you want. I'll make coffee, too." He couldn't normalize his voice, even though he tried, because he could see the way that Tom, and his mother, too, were looking at him.

"All right," his mother said. "Thank you."

After she left, Mike scraped the dishes and put them in the sink, making more noise than he needed to.

"Do you have a dish towel?" Tom asked. "I'll dry."

"I'll do it."

"I'm an old hand at doing dishes."

"So am I," Mike said.

Tom leaned casually against the counter, as if he didn't notice that Mike didn't want him there. "I eat at my brother's house a lot," he said. "Too much, probably. I do the dishes with Kyle, or his sister. My sister-in-law has to rest after dinner."

There was something wrong with Kyle's mother—Mike knew that but couldn't remember what it was. It was one of those background facts you knew about someone. Now he had one of his own: Mike Newlin's father killed somebody. Mike Newlin's father killed a woman he was having an affair with.

"She's in a wheelchair," Tom said. "She has ataxia. It's a disease that affects the nervous system."

"That's too bad," Mike said, sounding friendlier than he meant to.

"She's all right in every other way. Her family compensates for what she can't do. You know. They cover for her."

Mike put down the plate he was washing and looked at him. "Is this out of a psychology textbook?" he asked.

"Are you this suspicious of everything people say to you?"

"No," Mike said. "I'm not. Not with everybody." He got out two coffee mugs, ones his mother liked. They said: KISS THE TEACHER WHO HELPED YOU READ THIS.

"What's going to happen if you meet somebody smarter than you?" Tom asked.

"There are plenty of people smarter than I am."

"I'm not so sure about 'plenty.' "

"Don't bullshit me," Mike said. "That's what I hate. That's what makes me suspicious."

"So you'd be less suspicious if I said you weren't smart."

"You'd be too smart to say that," Mike said.

They stood less than two feet apart, not speaking. Mike poured water into the coffeemaker. Until the coffee began to brew, the only sound in the room was the rain falling outside.

"Mary Hise was smart, too," Tom said then. "Mostly A's in grade school, middle school, and the first two years of high school." He folded the wet dish towel and laid it on the counter. "Because," he said, "she got pregnant at sixteen. And the boyfriend didn't want anything to do with it. Or with her. That's what Mary's mother said."

"So things like that happen sometimes," Mike said.

Tom looked at him with his narrow eyes. "Don't you want to know what happened?"

"No," Mike said. "Or yes. Whatever." He was flustered; he'd been caught off guard. "I don't know. Whatever it is you expect me to say."

"I don't expect you to say anything in particular," Tom said calmly. "Anyway, she put it up for adoption." He shook his head, correcting himself. "I say 'it.' It was a girl, perfectly healthy."

He picked up the coffeepot. "You don't want any?" he asked Mike, and without waiting for an answer, he poured coffee into the two mugs Mike had set out. "You know what makes it so sad?" Tom said then to Mike. "That she'll never get a second chance. She'll never have a child she can keep as her own. That's what changes everything."

He went into the living room, and Mike was left in the kitchen alone, standing with his back against the counter. He felt terrible suddenly—not just terrible in the way that he imagined Tom wanted him to feel, but terrible beyond that, as if he had played a part in every bad thing that ever had happened to Mary Hise.

"Mike?" his mother called out from the next room. "Could you bring the milk and sugar?"

He carried those in and saw that Tom was sitting on the couch, next to her. She'd turned on only the standing lamp in the corner, which threw ghostly shadows onto the ceiling.

"This coffee smells good," Tom said. "I'm usually lazy and make myself instant."

Mike started to go upstairs, but his mother said, "Sit down for a minute."

"I have things to do."

"You can do them later."

He sat on the piano bench, next to a photograph of himself on Halloween. He'd been seven or so. He could remember his father taking it.

"I want to say what I started to say," his mother said, and he then could see how tense she still was. "I shouldn't have asked Mary Hise not to quit. I was afraid that Glenn might hurt himself. I never thought he would hurt Mary Hise. I could see that he loved her." Her voice had become high and distressed-sounding. She put her hands up to her face.

Mike was looking down at the piano keys. He was counting the black ones, hardly aware that he was doing it.

"Glenn had never hurt anyone before," Tom said.

"Everything about this was different from the way he was before," Carolyn said. "Maybe he'd never been in love before."

Mike felt shaky, even dizzy. Next to him was the photograph of himself, at seven, dressed in jeans and boots, with a metal star on his shirt: a sheriff, like in a Western movie. He'd wanted a holster and gun, but his mother had said no. Why not? his father had said. What's wrong with a gun if it's used to help people?

His mother was sitting still, her hands in her lap. She didn't seem to have more to say. Tom had his arm over the back of the couch, close to but not touching her. Outside, rain was still falling.

"I'm going to bed," Mike said, and left the room without looking again at either of them.

UPSTAIRS, he closed the door and sat on his bed in the dark. He used to do that after losing a wrestling match—just sit, not feeling sorry for himself but trying to believe that losing didn't matter. He wanted to call Donetta but knew that she'd gone to Keystone with her mother and sister. She liked the small shops and the tourists. She liked to drive past Mount Rushmore.

Finally Mike turned on his desk lamp and got out the road atlas his mother had bought him after he was accepted into South Dakota State. He looked up Salt Lake City. There were interstates leading away from it in four directions, but his father would have to be on one of those highways a long time before he'd get anywhere big. The bordering states were Nevada, Colorado, Wyoming, Idaho, Arizona, and New Mexico. He remembered a classmate who had moved to Wheatley from Phoenix. He remembered her saying, "Arizona's got a lot of old people and a lot of criminals."

Outside the thunder grew more distant. Mike's windows were open, and his brown curtains were being sucked in and pushed out by the wind. He turned off his lamp. After a while he heard the front door close and then a car door open and close: Tom DeWitt leaving.

So long, asshole, he thought, though a moment later he just felt sad. It seemed as if every man he knew was like his father—looking for a way to not be alone. It just wiped out whatever bad things men did. Then the next minute he

thought about Mary Hise, and about himself not thinking about Donetta even when she was going down on him,
and he saw everything from the opposite side—if men
were alone, then they shouldn't fuck up so much. They
shouldn't be such selfish assholes.

Mike heard his mother come up the stairs and stop outside his door. Don't even think about it, he said silently.
He heard her walk down the hall and go into her room. It
was after ten.

Mike undressed and got into bed. He used to sleep
naked, but he didn't do that anymore. He wore underwear
in case his mother should come into his room, or in case
something happened and he'd have to get up suddenly. A
lot of things were his responsibility now. Also, with underwear on he seemed to dream less about sex. He was too sexual, he thought. It was on his mind all the time, and he
wondered about things he'd read, connections there were
between male hormones and violence. He didn't feel like a
violent person. He'd never done anything violent, except
wrestling. He'd never even gone out for football.

He lay in bed, forgetting to put on his headphones so
that he wouldn't hear if his mother was crying. He didn't
care right now, anyway. But tonight he could hear her
opening drawers and moving hangers in the closet. She
wasn't doing it loudly. If he'd been asleep he wouldn't have
heard it; it wouldn't have woken him up. For just a moment he was afraid that she was leaving, too. Then he un-

derstood that she must be getting rid of his father's clothes.

He got up, put on his jeans, and went into her room. "What are you doing?" he said.

She didn't answer. She was piling his father's clothes into storage boxes she kept under the bed. There were more clothes than Mike had expected, even though his father had taken things with him. There were still pants, shirts, sweaters, and shoes.

"I want to think of him as dead," Mike's mother said.

The clothes were blurry now. Mike kept his back to his mother until his vision cleared, by which time she was crying. When he turned around, she was holding his father's blue shirt up to her face.

EIGHT

By the second week of July, there had been no more news about Mike's father, except that the district attorney had gotten an indictment against him, as Tom DeWitt had predicted. The search had intensified and was covering a bigger area. Though he might be in Canada by now, Mike's mother had said, or Mexico. But Mike didn't think so. His father wasn't courageous enough to escape to another country.

Mike and his mother began not to talk about the situation directly. The truth was that Mike and his mother didn't talk much anymore, period. Carolyn started tutoring students in the evening, and Mike started working more hours at the Schofield ranch—six days a week and sometimes seven.

"It wouldn't hurt you to be home more often," his

mother said to him early on a Saturday morning. The temperature had been in the upper nineties, and the kitchen was already hot, flies buzzing against the screen door.

"What about you?" Mike said. "Look at how much you're working."

"I've always been responsible for everything in this family. Maybe you just never noticed before."

"Thanks for reminding me."

"I'm sorry. But I'm not going to lie about it." She shoved her chair back, getting up to make Mike more pancakes, though he hadn't asked for them. "I'm tutoring people who want to improve their lives," she said then. She mentioned an adult student named Jim Reynolds, and how enthusiastic he was about being back in school. "He doesn't just sit there and expect me to do all the work."

Like Dad, Mike thought, noticing how, now that they didn't talk about his father directly, his mother couldn't let a sentence just be a sentence. Everything had to be an indirect reference to something his father had or hadn't done—even before he'd gotten involved with Mary Hise. His father had screwed up in other ways; Mike knew that. More often than not he'd been difficult to be around. He hadn't been successful at his job, and he hadn't helped out much around the house, either, or with Mike, when Mike was young. His parents always had been unequal, Mike knew; they'd been like an unbalanced seesaw. His mother had been the one to keep his father up, keep him going. Without her, his father might have come crashing down. But what about his father's side of things, Mike wondered. What would it feel like if your family didn't have faith in you?

He watched his mother eat. He could tell by looking at her that she wasn't sleeping enough. The skin under her eyes was dark, and she looked exhausted first thing in the morning. She probably didn't feel all that great, either. But he didn't want to think about that. If he did, he'd feel sorry for her, which would be like giving in, somehow. Having it be just the two of them now made the tension between them more obvious. Neither one of them wanted to give in, on anything. They were alike, Mike thought, whereas Mike's father had been a completely different kind of person from either of them—more emotional, less reliable. Mike's father had been in the middle, between Mike and his mother, more than Mike had been in the middle, between his parents. Mike had never understood that before.

"What are you thinking so hard about?" his mother said.

"I don't know. Nothing," he told her. "The heat."

LATER in the day, at the Schofields', Mike felt tired and slow. While standing in the shade with Lee-Ann, who was waiting for a new couch to be delivered, he drank two Cokes to wake himself up. Neil was nearby, showing Janna the baby rabbits.

"She wants to play with them," Lee-Ann said. "She doesn't understand that they're just babies." The wind blew through her brown hair, redder now from the sun,

Mike noticed, though her skin was still white. She was wearing a sleeveless dress so thin and light that he could see her slender legs through the fabric.

They watched the furniture truck turn into the long gravel driveway. "There's nothing wrong with our old couch," Lee-Ann told Mike, "except that we're sick of it. I know how spoiled we must sound to you." It was the "our" and the "we" again that Mike hated.

"It's not like I live in a trailer," he said. "You have the right to get new furniture if you want."

"You're right," she said. "I'm sorry. I didn't mean anything by it." And Mike regretted having said anything.

It was Neil who asked Mike if he'd help Lee-Ann rearrange furniture. "She's always wanting to move things around," he said. "It drives me crazy. So this time it's your turn." Before heading down the hill toward the barn, he kissed Lee-Ann, and Mike thought that Lee-Ann seemed shy, suddenly, knowing that Mike was watching.

Inside, she put Janna down for her nap, then in the living room, with Mike's help, tried every possible furniture combination. "That probably seemed silly to you," she told him afterward.

"Why do you keep worrying about what I think?" Mike said. "It's like you think I'm judging you all the time."

"I care about what you think," Lee-Ann said.

She got him an iced tea, and they sat on the screened-in porch. Lee-Ann asked him how things were at home.

"Okay," he said. "Strange."

He saw the tractor far in the distance, with Louis Ivy on it; in front of the barn Neil and Ed were looking at the engine of Ed's old Corvette. Watching them, Mike felt homesick for the way he used to feel about the Schofields, when he was younger, when he'd looked up to them and wanted to be like them. He was too old to have those kinds of feelings now. And his view of the Schofields had altered, first because of his father's attitude toward Neil, then because of his own attraction to Lee-Ann.

"We packed up my father's stuff," he told Lee-Ann now. "My mom went through the house and packed away everything that was his."

"Did that make her feel better?"

"I'm not sure about better. Different, maybe."

"That must have been hard."

"I guess," Mike said. "I don't know. We just did it."

"You're so cool about it. You don't have to be that way with me."

"I'm not being any way with you," Mike said. He watched her lift her hair and hold it up from her neck. Her skin was damp from the heat. "You're the one who's not the same with me anymore," he said quietly.

She got up and stood with her back to him, looking down the hill toward the pond. "Too many things have changed," she said.

"Okay," Mike said. "But don't tell me I'm the one who should be different." She didn't speak or turn around, and he looked at her dress, the material thin enough for him to know almost exactly what she would look like without it.

"You can change the way you act, you know, without changing the way you feel," Lee-Ann said.

"Why would you want to?"

She turned to look at him. "Because," she said. Then, "I don't know. I think what you need is a friend."

"I have friends," Mike said.

They watched Neil and Ed get into the Corvette and drive it out onto the highway.

"Who besides Josh?" Lee-Ann said. Mike was glad that she didn't mention Donetta.

"I don't know," he said. "Do you want a list?"

"Just give me one name."

"Dave," Mike said.

"Dave who?"

"You mean they have to have last names?"

"Most real people do," Lee-Ann told him.

"You mean they have to be real?"

She smiled a little. "Real is the minimum requirement. Anyway, when was the last time you talked to Josh?"

"Three days ago," Mike lied.

"Really?"

"Why would I lie about it?"

"Well, that's good then." She stood next to the wicker rocker, the breeze stirring her dress. "Don't you think I have a point, though?" she asked in that sweeter, more intimate voice. "Don't you think that what I'm saying makes sense?"

"It's not about sense," Mike said. "I don't think about sense when I look at you."

Her face and neck flushed. She looked toward the inside of the house, as if she'd heard Janna wake. Then she looked at Mike flirtatiously, the way she used to. "What do you think about when you look at me?" she asked him, and Mike got up and reached for her. He felt the dampness of her dress and her cool hands on the back of his neck, and this time she didn't move away from him. She moved closer, and he put his hands on her hips, then under the dress. But when he kissed her, finally, after imagining for a year what it would be like, he was sick and had to push her away and hurry inside, down the hall to the bathroom. He shut the door behind him and sat on the floor, sweaty and cold, too dizzy to stand up. He leaned his forehead against the cool, porcelain bathtub and listened to Lee-Ann's footsteps coming down the hall.

"Mike?" she said. "Are you all right?"

"I'm sick," he said. "I have the flu." Then he lay down on the tile floor, feeling worse about himself than he could ever remember.

When he came out she led him into the kitchen. "Sit down," she said, and placed a glass of 7-Up in front of him. "It's good for your stomach." She sat across from him, her elbows on the table. "That was my fault. I don't know what I was thinking. I wasn't thinking."

"No," he told her. "I was just sick."

"Sick since when?" Lee-Ann said.

"I don't know. Yesterday."

"Thanks for sharing your germs with me." When Mike didn't even smile, she said, "Well, here's my excuse. I missed your paying attention to me."

"You're kidding."

"Do you think I'm too old to care about things like that?"

"Like I think thirty is old?" Mike said.

"Well, some people do. I bet your friends do."

"My friends are smarter than that."

Lee-Ann was watching him from across the table. "Things don't always have to be physical," she said. "You don't always have to do something. You can be close to people without even moving. It can all take place in your head."

"That's not the same kind of close," Mike said.

"It's a good kind, though. Maybe it would be good for you."

"Like medicine."

"See?" Lee-Ann said. "You can't really even picture it." She poured him more 7-Up, her soft hair falling forward against her cheek. "Do you know what I worry about?" she said to him. "That when you're my age you'll look back and wonder what kind of person I must have been."

"No," Mike said. "I'll just know I was lucky."

He finished his drink and left the cool house for the hot afternoon outside. He was already replaying in his mind what had happened and trying to make it different, like

maybe he did have the flu—though he felt all right now—
or maybe he'd been afraid that Neil and Ed would drive up
at that moment and see them together. Lee-Ann shouldn't
have taken that chance, he thought. She shouldn't have
made him that nervous. She shouldn't have made him wait
so long to begin with.

MIKE worked alone after that. Neil and Ed returned, and
Mike washed and waxed the Corvette, then cleaned out a
dark, clammy corner of the barn, which reminded him, in a
depressing way, of the cellar in his grandparents' house—
his father's parents, who had died, one after the other, the
year Mike was eleven. They'd lived in a one-story frame
house on the eastern edge of town; Mike's grandfather had
had a small welding business. When Mike thought of their
house, he thought of his father going down into the cellar
for a box of old toys for Mike to play with. He remembered
the ugly way his grandparents had talked to each other, and
then the nice way they'd talked to Mike and Mike's parents,
as if that niceness were a kind of punishment for each other.

Mike's father had been the only person in the family to
attend college. Glenn's brother, Randall, who had enlisted
and stayed in the army, was stationed in Germany. They
weren't close. Mike hardly knew him, and Mike's mother
had waited weeks before contacting him. "I don't have anything to say about it," Randall had said. "There was always
something wrong with his personality."

"How helpful," Mike's mother had said afterward. "I'm
sorry I called him."

IT was five o'clock by the time Mike finished. He needed
to be home earlier than usual—Donetta had invited him to
a family barbecue that night. Her grandmother was visit-
ing from Pierre, along with the grandmother's new boyfriend. Before Mike left the Schofields', however, he went
up to the house, where Lee-Ann was sitting on the front
steps with Janna.

"I've thought about what happened," he said. "I understand it now." In a lower voice he added, "Let's go inside
for a minute."

"You don't have to prove it to me. I believe you."

"I'm not trying to prove anything."

She looked at him the way his mother did sometimes—
as if she knew more about him than he did, and he said
good-bye, turned around, and walked quickly down the
hill to his motorcycle. He put on his helmet and rode out
of the long driveway too fast, skidding on the gravel, and
on the way home he planned how to act the next time he
saw her—as if this day hadn't happened. Then he would
gradually start flirting with her again, so that before long
they could get back to where they used to be with each
other, back in May. Then he could kiss her for real. She'd
be able to see, then, how much he'd always wanted to. But
first he had to act as if it were no big deal. He thought

about calling her as soon as he got home, pretending that he'd forgotten to tell Neil something so that she could see that his mind was already on other things. He just needed to think of a reason to call that would make sense.

By the time he was back in Wheatley, though, on Edge Street, he was too tired to think about it any longer. He was tired of having to make things all right all the time, of having to act a certain way so that somebody would think of him a certain way, or so that he could fix something he screwed up. He wished he could just make a mistake once in a while, he thought, as he rode his motorcycle up the driveway and into the carport. Then he saw his father's disorganized workbench and thought, If you let yourself make mistakes, how do you keep them small? How do you keep worse ones from happening?

He took off his helmet and began to organize his father's tools.

NINE

CORY Burris was cooking a pig in a hole in the Rushes' backyard. He'd dug the pit early that morning, without asking for Mrs. Rush's permission, and when Mike rode up the driveway, Mrs. Rush was standing out front near the juniper bushes, talking on her portable phone. Mike cut off his motorcycle engine in time to hear her say, "It's not like he dug it with a spoon, Pastor Kelly. I could bury my mother in that hole."

She gestured for Mike to go into the house. The only person inside was Margo, in the kitchen, drinking a wine cooler as she made potato salad. "Donetta's out back," she said, drying her tears with a paper napkin. "I don't know why there has to be this kind of trouble all the time. I think people should try to be peaceful with each other."

Mike went through the living room and out the sliding

glass door into the early-evening light. Donetta was sitting on a lawn chair next to her grandmother and her grandmother's boyfriend, a short, elderly man with glasses.

"Here's my sweetheart," Donetta said, when Mike appeared. She got up and kissed him. "This is Grandma Sharp and her friend, Wilbert Greenway." Mike shook hands with Mr. Greenway and said hello to Donetta's grandmother, whom he'd been warned about. "She's not mentally ill exactly," Donetta had told him, "but she can be mean enough to make you cry."

"We've heard all about you," Donetta's grandmother said. "We know everything, and Donetta said not to bring it up. But I don't agree with that."

"Thanks a lot," Donetta told her.

"I believe in being straightforward," her grandmother said.

"You're going to college in the fall?" Wilbert asked kindly.

"South Dakota State," Mike told him.

"In the honors program," Donetta said. "He gets better grades than I do."

Cory waved to Mike from the back of the yard, which was already in shadow, and Mike walked across the thick, green grass, watered daily in the summer unless it rained. That was Donetta's job. "Personally I don't care if it turns blue," she'd told Mike more than once.

Cory was standing guard over the pit, in which a pig,

wrapped in heavy tinfoil, was buried in coals. "Isn't this something?" he said. "I've wanted to do this for years." Behind him was a cooler filled with Cokes and beer. He got a beer for Mike and opened one for himself.

"She's pissed off, though," he told Mike, meaning his mother-in-law, Mike knew, whose name was not in Cory's vocabulary. "I can't blame her really—I did fuck up the lawn—but I hate how she makes Margo feel. She tries to come between us that way." He looked across the lush lawn. "There's a thing in the Bible about that," he told Mike. " 'Let no man put asunder.' It means you have to respect your in-laws."

"She's into having a nice house and yard," Mike said. "Donetta said she grew up in a trailer park."

"Well, nice grass is one thing," Cory said. "But a marriage is a lot more important."

Mrs. Rush was coming outside now, followed by Donetta's heavyset aunt, Nancy, and Nancy's daughter, Ellen. They lived in Spearfish, and Mike had met them before. The daughter was four years older than he was and always wore a camouflage army jacket, no matter what the weather. She'd failed junior college and was rejected by the army; now she worked as a security guard at an office building in Rapid City. "They almost gave her a gun," Donetta had told Mike. "Then they came to their senses."

Donetta kissed her aunt and walked toward Mike and Cory. She had on a short yellow dress and sandals with straps that wound around the ankle. When she saw Mike watching her, she smiled the way she had the first time she'd ever seen him—as if she'd never smile that way again for anybody else. Cory got her a Coke.

"I'm sorry about Grandma Sharp," she told Mike. "We didn't tell her anything. Wilbert's hobby is reading newspapers."

"They're leaving tomorrow, right?" Cory said. "Isn't that what they promised?" He waved to Margo, who came outside carrying the bowl of potato salad. "My beautiful baby is finally here," he told Mike. He poked at the coals, peeled back the tinfoil, and inspected the pig's head.

THEY ate outside at a long wooden table Cory had made out of leftover lumber from a Rapid City subdivision. Mike figured he'd gotten the lumber, unknowingly, from somebody who'd stolen it. Cory wasn't smart, but he wasn't a thief, either. He brought over a huge platter of pork.

"This is delicious," Donetta's aunt said.

"There's nothing wrong with pork cooked in the kitchen," Mrs. Rush said.

"What you need is a cook-off," Wilbert told her. "Invite the neighbors and see who likes what best."

"No, thank you," Mrs. Rush said.

"Do you even know the neighbors?" Grandma Sharp asked.

"Of course I know the neighbors."

"The lawns here are so gigantic," Grandma Sharp said. "You'd need a go-cart to get from one house to the next."

"It's a beautiful area," Wilbert said.

"People go up to their ears in debt to live in these houses," Grandma Sharp told him. "They go into debt so that they can clean rooms they never go into."

"That's hardly how we live," Mrs. Rush said. "Our house is too crowded, if anything."

"Is that right?" Margo said. "Well, it doesn't have to be anymore."

Everyone ate in silence. Under the table Donetta had her hand on Mike's leg. All she was eating for dinner was potato salad, bread, and olives. "I'm not going to eat any pork," she'd told Mike earlier. "Pigs remind me of Wilbur, in *Charlotte's Web*."

For dessert there were berry cobblers that Donetta's aunt had brought. It was nearly dark, and Margo lit candles. Donetta's cousin Ellen ran around the darkening yard, catching fireflies with her hands.

"We had family picnics like this when I was growing up," Wilbert said. "It was during the Depression. My dad would cook hot dogs. Wieners, we called them."

"Were the picnics happy?" Margo asked.

"Sure," Wilbert said.

"Maybe things you remember just seem happy," Margo told him.

"I remember bad things, too, honey."

"Grandma?" Donetta said. "What kinds of things do you remember?"

"I don't like rummaging around in the past," Grandma Sharp said. "It's over and done with."

Mrs. Rush picked up a candle, crossed the pretty lawn, and looked down at the pit. She nudged a little dirt back in with her shoe.

LATER, Mike and Donetta took a walk through the small subdivision and into the field on the other side of Flat Rock Road. The moon was up, so white and shining that they could see deer paths in the long grass.

"I think about this field when I can't get to sleep at night," Donetta said. "I imagine I'm lying in it with you."

"You think about me too much," Mike said.

She let go of his hand. "Who should I think about, then?"

"Well, nobody, really. You should think about yourself and what you want."

"What do you think I want?" Donetta said.

There was silence. Then they could hear, in the distance, firecrackers Cory was setting off in the Rushes' backyard.

"I don't know," Mike said finally. "Me, I guess."

"But I shouldn't say it, right? Because it makes you feel trapped, and you worry about what's going to happen to me when you go away to college."

"Yes," Mike said.

Donetta stood apart from him in the darkness. Mike

knew she was crying, though she wasn't moving or making a sound. When her father had died, she'd cried silently like that, as if she'd not expected to be comforted.

"I'm not trying to be an asshole," he said.

"Then don't be one."

He put his hands on her shoulders, looking down at her wet face.

"Are you breaking up with me?" she asked him.

"No. I don't know what I'm doing."

"You always know what you're doing."

"I used to," Mike said. "I used to think I did." He touched her face and hair, and when she didn't respond, he dropped his hands and lay down in the grass, just as he'd lain down in Lee Ann's bathroom that afternoon.

"You're going to get chigger bites," Donetta told him.

"I know. I don't care."

He closed his eyes, and after a moment heard her lie down next to him. The firecrackers had stopped, and from across the street they heard voices, then a car leaving. "Aunt Nancy and Ellen," Donetta said sadly.

Mike leaned over and kissed her. It was a test for him, at first—given what had happened earlier with Lee-Ann—until Donetta began to kiss him back. She slid her hands up under his shirt and caressed his shoulders and chest; she stroked his erection. As he unzipped his jeans he watched her lift up her dress and take it off. He positioned her on top of him, so that he could see her body in the moonlight. For the first time Mike was thinking only of her, even from the beginning, and though he didn't say that he loved her, he could have said it without lying.

Afterward he reached up and touched her long hair, and the necklace she always wore—a small gold heart on a gold chain, a present from her father. His hands were trembling, and he felt the edge of something hiding inside him: the fear of what it might be like if Donetta didn't love him.

"Let's get up," he whispered. He stood, tucking in his shirt, and led Donetta through the field. He felt better then, but he wanted to get back to where he could see lights and houses, and the shadowy, familiar outline of the Black Hills in the distance. He and Donetta stopped at the edge of the road, from where they could see Mrs. Rush and her mother in the big, lighted kitchen window. Donetta's grandmother was drying a butcher knife.

"Your family's screwed up," Mike said.

"I know. My father was the only nice one."

"No," Mike told her. "The nice one is standing next to me."

IT was after ten when he rode up Edge Street. He'd expected his house to be dark and his mother asleep, but from a block away he could see lit-up windows and a car out front—Tom DeWitt's, he recognized as he got closer. Something had happened with his father.

He left the motorcycle in the driveway and went into the house wearing his helmet. In the kitchen, standing at the table, his mother and Tom were looking down at a map of Kansas.

"There's been a close call," Carolyn said. "But they don't know where he is."

Mike's father had been seen in a Jeep, with a woman, stopped on the side of Interstate 70 between Denver and Kansas City—a Jeep Cherokee with a Colorado license plate. They had a small dog with them, Tom said. Mary Ilise's dog, almost certainly. Ten miles west of Oakley, Kansas, heading toward Kansas City, they'd had car trouble and were looking under the hood—a spark plug had come loose. A Kansas state patrolman had pulled up behind them and asked if they needed help. That was three hours ago now. Routinely, he'd called in the license plate; the car was registered to the woman.

"That's why he didn't check Glenn's identification," Tom said to Mike. "There was no reason to. But afterward, the patrolman had a feeling about it. He said that the man had seemed nervous, and that he'd let the woman do all the talking. By this time half an hour had gone by. He checked with the dispatcher, found out about the ATL—Attempt to Locate—and gave her the license plate and description of the Jeep. But it hasn't been seen since. They must have gotten off the highway. Western Kansas is an empty place, but Glenn was in a vehicle that could go anywhere. We had a chance and messed it up."

He folded up the map and helped himself to a glass of water. It was hot and still outside, and there'd been heat lightning as Mike had ridden home. Mike watched Tom set the glass on the table, then rethink that and place it in the sink. There was nothing he did, Mike thought, that he didn't do deliberately.

"Why are you telling us this?" Mike asked him.

"Don't you want to know?"

"Of course we do," Carolyn said.

"You should keep it to yourselves, though," Tom said. "It's not something you'll see in the newspaper."

"Then you shouldn't have told us," Mike said.

"Don't be so difficult," his mother told him. "Would you rather not know?"

Tom rested his hands, casually, on the back of a chair. "I'll tell you why I told you. I thought you might have the same concern we have. That your father might harm this woman."

"He won't," Mike said.

His mother said, "There's no reason to worry about her. Glenn hates himself for what he's done."

"How do you know that?" Tom said.

"Because he hated himself before he did it."

Mike turned away from them. That was bullshit, he thought. It was the kind of thing people said on talk shows. And it was too personal a thing to say. For the last eighteen years his mother had felt fine being private about private things. But now that his father was hiding, his mother was doing the opposite, revealing things about both herself and

Mike's father. Mike wondered what kinds of things she'd been telling Tom DeWitt about him—Mike.

"I'm putting my motorcycle away," he told them, and went outside. He wheeled his bike into the carport, and as he hung up his helmet he thought about the fact that his father wasn't hiding alone anymore. Mike had been able to imagine what it might feel like to be alone and in trouble. He couldn't picture his father that same way now.

He stood in the dark driveway, watching his mother and Tom DeWitt through the window. They were sitting down, talking, both of them leaning forward in their chairs. Mike's mother's hair was a little longer and less neat than it used to be—a more ordinary length—and her red sleeveless blouse was open at the neck. Sitting there under the kitchen light, they both seemed more substantial to Mike than Mike seemed to himself. They were sharp-edged and vivid, whereas he felt like a shadow. Why couldn't he seem that definite to himself? Why didn't he feel that solid? Why couldn't he see himself as clearly as he could see them?

He stayed outside and walked—down Edge Street to Pine and up Arapahoe, where Josh used to live and where Josh's mother lived now with her boyfriend. If Josh were around, Mike thought, the two of them could take off for a few days, go to a rodeo in Wyoming, or go camping in the Hills. Josh was always up to something adventurous, and often illegal. In the fall he was going to the University of

South Dakota in Sioux Falls, on a football scholarship, and he'd said once to Mike, "I'm trying not to get arrested before that."

And that made Mike think of the university he would be attending, and of the visit he'd made there last fall, with his parents. There had been an away football game that weekend, and everybody in Brookings had seemed to be crowded into bars and restaurants, watching the game on television.

"You'll get caught up in that, too," Mike's father had told him. "Don't think you won't. You'll be shouting along with the rest of the idiots." He'd gotten into a bad mood then, and Mike and his mother had ended up walking around the deserted campus by themselves.

Mike was back on Edge Street, all the houses dark except his own. He waited at a distance, away from the streetlight, until Tom DeWitt drove off.

TEN

WYLENE Moseley was the name of the woman his father had been with, and might be with still. She was a waitress from Central City, Colorado, a town in the mountains west of Denver. She was forty-two years old.

"I can tell you what she looks like," Tom DeWitt told Mike on the phone, Monday morning, during a thunderstorm that had begun at dawn and kept Mike home. "My mother's teaching," Mike had said at first, when Tom had called, and Tom had said, "I know. I thought just you and I could talk."

"Blue eyes and black hair," he said now. "Five seven, a hundred forty pounds. Attractive features. Is that how you pictured her?"

"I didn't picture her."

"But you must have wondered."

Mike knew better than to say he had. All day Sunday, as he and his mother had waited for a phone call telling them that his father had been arrested, or worse, they'd never once mentioned the woman. She'd become unmentionable—like an untouchable in India, Mike thought, which was a bad joke, because he knew that his father would be touching her.

"Have you heard her name before?" Tom asked.

"No."

"Do you think she's somebody your father knew?"

"I don't know," Mike said.

"My guess is that he met her on the road, somehow, and that she knows he's in trouble."

Mike was on the phone in the upstairs hallway, from where he could see his mother's neatly made bed and the window beyond it. "Why would she go with him, then?" he said coolly, as if he didn't care, really.

"Do you know who gets the most letters in prison?" Tom said. "Men who've murdered women." When Mike said nothing, Tom said, "I don't understand it either. But I can tell you what I think she thinks—that your father's been treated unfairly. Also, she likes danger. Adrenaline makes her feel more alive—that kind of thing."

"It makes everybody feel that way."

"Some people feel good and alive the second they wake up in the morning."

"Like you?" Mike said.

"Never. Do you?"

"No."

"We have something in common, then," Tom said. "We have something else in common, too. We don't want to see this woman get hurt."

"So?" Mike said.

"It's just something we share, like the way we wish Mary Hise hadn't died."

"Everybody wishes that."

"You must wish it especially," Tom said. "You knew her."

That was true, which was the meanest thing about it. Mike stood in the dim hallway for a long time after they hung up, looking through his mother's window at the dark sky and falling rain. Finally he got out the vacuum cleaner, as his mother had asked him to, and started downstairs, pushing it hard into the corners, angry at himself for answering the phone to begin with or for not saying: You think you're being clever, making me feel bad about Mary Hise? How could I not feel bad about her?

Upstairs, he did his mother's room, his own room, and the small, oblong guest room, which had a window overlooking the backyard. Then he turned off the vacuum cleaner and sat on the old four-poster bed that had belonged to his great-grandmother. The guest room was where he and Donetta had had sex whenever his parents had been out of town. Often, Mike would walk past the room, look at the bed, and remember exactly how Donetta had looked, naked on the white sheets. An unused room was sexual the way a motel room was, Mike thought.

Never occupied long enough by any one person, it was emptier than empty, like a pool without water, or sleep without dreams.

Mike's father was probably staying in motels with Wy- lene Moseley—if that was even her name, Mike thought, if Tom DeWitt hadn't made up the name, or even the whole story. But if she was real, Mike knew, his father was sleep- ing with her, because if he'd slept with Mary Hise, then he'd sleep with other women as well. That was how Mike was himself, in a way, and he felt too depressed right then to imagine that he could be different. He wondered if Wy- lene Moseley knew about Mike and his mother, or about Mary Hise; he wondered how his father had gotten her to help him. His father acted differently around attractive women. The first few times Donetta had come over for dinner, for example, he'd cleared the table, carried in dessert, and stood when Donetta got up from her chair. He'd been overly friendly and polite around some of Mike's mother's friends, as well. Women had always seemed to like him more than men had, at least at first. Donetta had liked him a lot, until she got to know him better. Then she'd said to Mike, "I get tired of paying at- tention to him."

Outside, in back, rain was pooling in the low spots under the crab-apple tree. Mike had filled in those hollows with dirt, then peat moss, but they formed themselves again each time it rained. There were things you couldn't change, including things about yourself, Mike thought; he was bad at being faithful, and women—girls—liked him, too. He knew how to make them like him.

He stood at the window, imagining what Wylene Moseley must be like, taking off with his father like that. She was probably an outdoors kind of person—the kind of person Mike was more than his father was, although his father never would have admitted that. Mike had seen pictures of him hiking in national parks, but his father had never backpacked anywhere, or climbed a real mountain, or even stayed in a tent for more than one night.

Mike remembered that when he was five or six, his father had set up a small yellow tent for him and Josh in the backyard. "You boys will have a lot of fun out here," Glenn had told them. "You'll be like cowboys." He'd gotten them sleeping bags and settled them out there after dark. Then later, after a dog barked and an animal got into the trash, he came outside and knelt at the tent's opening. "Are you scared?" he'd asked kindly. "Do you want to come in?"

"No," they'd told him.

"Stay out all night, then," he'd said coldly, and gone inside.

AT noon, Mike's mother came home for lunch, shaking off her umbrella on the patio and bringing into the kitchen the smell of rain. "Were there any calls?" she asked.

"No," he said, lying so that he didn't seem so involved, somehow. Tom DeWitt kept doing that to him, Mike thought—creating secrets between the two of them, and even when Mike could see it coming, he didn't seem able to stop it. It just kept happening.

"That's good, I suppose," his mother said, taking a pot of soup from the refrigerator and heating it up on the stove. She turned around and smiled at Mike. "I had a good class this morning. You know how I judge that? Because when there's ten minutes left I suddenly remember what I have to come home to—the situation, I mean."

"That happens to me sometimes," Mike said, relieved that she was referring to it. "I'll forget about it for a while." He moved aside his mother's books in order to set the table.

"Some of those are for you," she said, "from your list. I got them out of the library." Mike's high school guidance counselor had given book lists to everyone going on to college.

"Just don't make me read them."

"What?" his mother said sharply.

"It's a joke," he told her. "It's what Cory Burris said about a book Mrs. Rush tried to hit him with."

His mother wasn't smiling anymore. "I worry about you spending time over there," she said.

"That's ridiculous."

"I guess it is," she said. "I guess it's Mrs. Rush who should worry about Donetta coming over here. It must seem funny to people now, what a snob I was."

"I didn't say that."

"I know you didn't. But it was implied in what you said."

They ate lunch without speaking further. It was useless to talk to her, Mike thought, even though she'd come home in a good mood. Things he thought were funny she didn't; she was always trying to be the parent. She couldn't sit there and just listen.

He washed the dishes as she got her books together. "I have an afternoon class," she said. "Then a tutoring session with Jim Reynolds and two others. Jim Reynolds is the only one I look forward to." She put a lipstick into her purse and came toward Mike as if she wanted to hug him good-bye. When he kept his hands busy with the dishes, she hesitated, then opened the door. A few minutes later he heard her backing the car down the driveway.

MIKE slept most of the afternoon. He dreamed of a rainy night in which his father was being chased through a corn-field with Lucky, their dog that had been killed so long ago. There was a woman with him. There was a building in the distance, a cross between a silo and a prison, and Lucky was half running, half flying. Close by on a playground, a kid was hanging by one hand from the top of a slide. Mike woke up sweating.

It was five-thirty, and the rain had stopped. The house was silent and empty. He got on his motorcycle and rode through town on the wet streets, past his father's insurance agency, which now had STUART WELLS written on the door, past the apartment where Mary Hise had lived, and north on County Road 51 to Little Falls Park, where Mary used to go with her dog.

The park consisted of hay fields and cottonwoods, and a rocky stream wound through it. Some summers it dried up completely, but now it was shallow with rain. Mike walked along the gravel path. During his freshman year, he'd been a member of the track team, and the coach had driven them out there to run. Mike wasn't fast enough and didn't focus, according to his coach. He'd just run and think. He'd solve math problems in his head. At the end of the season he quit the team but kept on running, and Donetta started running with him. "So I get to spend more time with you," she had said. Even from the beginning she'd made it clear to Mike how much he meant to her.

"You shouldn't do that," he'd told her. "It makes you easy to take advantage of."

"Why would you take advantage of me?" she'd asked.

She didn't understand, still, that you should always hold back, keep part of yourself to yourself. Otherwise, you'd be affected by external things all the time—by what people said and did, by the way they acted toward you. You'd be like a rootless tree, Mike thought, too shallow to live. His father had been like that. That was why his father had cried all night when the dog died. That was why he'd taken an overdose of pills when his college girlfriend broke up with him. Mike thought about that incident now, as he walked along the path. Did his father think that trying to kill himself would bring the girlfriend back? Because why would you want somebody who didn't want you?

The sky began to clear before dusk, the clouds dissipating and the horizon peach-colored and bright. The fields were golden green from the rain. A woman came toward Mike, jogging, her Border collie running behind her.

Mary Hise will never see this park again, he thought. She'll never have another dog. She'll never pose for another picture.

He walked until it was too dark to see across the field. He tried to keep his mind blank, but thoughts about Mary came into it, serious ones: the baby she'd had; how uncertain she'd looked in her high school photograph; the fact that she'd died alone.

Mike kept walking, just looking at the darkness.

ELEVEN

JOSH Mitchell came back to Wheatley on a Sunday at the end of July. He had a court hearing to go to: Duane King had attacked his mother. He'd broken her wrist and bruised her face, and Josh was scheduled to testify. He'd seen him threaten her once. "It was a few weeks before my dad and I moved," he told Mike Sunday night. "I kicked him in the balls."

"Why didn't you tell me?"

"I was too pissed off to talk about it." After a moment he added, "She was nuts to be with him."

It was after dark, and they were at Crow Lake, sitting in Josh's car with the doors open, drinking beer and waiting for Donetta and Josh's ex-girlfriend, Pam, to drive out and meet them. It wasn't certain that Pam would come. She was dating somebody else now, somebody older, from

Spearfish. And she was supposedly still angry at Josh for breaking up with her last winter.

"She expected me to marry her or some bullshit like that," Josh said now. "So I told her to back off and get real, and she punched me."

"You deserved it," Mike said.

"Why?"

"I don't know. I'm just quoting Donetta."

"Donetta hates me," Josh said.

"Hate's a strong word. Detest might be closer." Mike opened another beer and put his bare foot up on the cracked dashboard. Josh's car was an old, beat-up Lincoln his father had traded an ancient Airstream for. Josh's father was a geologist, but he also collected junk that he sold or traded for more junk. Josh's mother had wanted him to get out of that business. They'd fought constantly. It was no surprise to Mike that they got divorced. The surprise was that Josh's mother had been sneaking around with Duane King, who already had three ex-wives. Mike and Josh had gone to school with his son, who everybody figured would end up in prison.

"Do you think Pam'll come?" Josh asked.

"Donetta will. I don't know about Pam."

Josh got out of the car and took off his T-shirt and jeans. He walked in the darkness to the edge of the lake, dove in, and swam underwater until he was out deep.

"This feels so fucking good," he yelled to Mike.

Mike had gone swimming earlier, when they'd first gotten there. He'd worked with Neil and Ed all day, and the temperature had been up to 104. Lee-Ann had come out of the house once, in cutoff jeans and the top of a two-piece bathing suit. Mike had gotten an erection as soon as he saw her. He'd felt like unzipping his jeans right there, in front of her husband and brother-in-law, to prove to her that he was okay again, and as attracted to her as ever. It was such a crazy thought that it scared him. It made him think that anybody could become crazy just by doing a crazy thing. It could happen in a second if you let it.

Mike heard Donetta's car. He got out, stood behind a tree, then jumped out in front of her headlights.

"I knew you'd do that," she said. "I just said that to Pam."

"She did," Pam said.

They had carry-out boxes with them from Andell's Diner—cheeseburgers, onion rings, and Cokes. Donetta spread a blanket on the ground between the cars, and Pam said hello to Mike. She didn't ask where Josh was. She and Mike had been friends in high school; they'd sat next to each other in advanced calculus and worked together on the problems. She was tall and long-legged, with large breasts and a pretty face. She looked older than she was.

"Hey," Josh said. They couldn't see him, but they could hear his footsteps. He went behind the car to put on his jeans.

"So what's going on?" Pam said in a less-than-friendly way.

"Nothing," he told her. "Everything. A lot of shit has happened."

"No kidding," Mike said.

"I don't mean just that," Josh said. "Things seem different, like I've been gone for years. I don't know why. Maybe it's just me. It probably is. It's probably just me being weird like I get sometimes." He was talking rapidly. For as long as Mike had known him, people had thought of Josh as cocky, but to Mike he'd always seemed more nervous than people realized.

"I'm sorry about your mother," Pam said. "I always liked her."

"She's not dead," Josh said. "I mean, it spooks me to hear you say it like that."

"I was just being polite."

"Okay. That's okay then." Josh took a breath, and they sat down on the blanket to eat. "I'm hungry as shit," Josh said. "Thanks, Donetta. I'll pay you for it."

"Forget it." It was the first thing Donetta had said to him. She was leaning back against Mike, her legs outstretched between his. She'd once told Mike that when it came to girls Josh was like dynamite—dangerous at a distance, deadly up close.

"Donetta gets a discount, even for take-out," Mike told Josh.

"It was still nice of her to think of it," Josh said.

"I'm a nice person," Donetta said.

The night was hot and hazy—a few stars but no moon,

and lightning too far in the distance for them to hear thunder.

"My dad said to tell you hi," Pam said to Josh. "Can you believe it? He started liking you the second you stopped liking me."

"What second was that?" Josh said. "Because I must have missed it. I don't remember it happening."

No one spoke. Donetta took Mike's hand. After a minute they got up and left Josh and Pam alone. They found their way down the dark trail to the water, undressed, and swam halfway out into the lake. They were both strong swimmers, but Mike was faster. He got there a minute or so before she did and waited for her to catch up. Then they headed for the bank on their left and pulled themselves up onto a limestone ledge that jutted out over the water. They lay close to each other in the darkness.

"You should give Josh a chance," Mike said.

"Why?"

"Because it's not like you not to."

Donetta was silent. Then she said, "That's a mean thing to say. It's like saying, 'You're proving you're not as good a person as you think you are.' You're not even thinking about the way Josh is. You just make it all about me."

"You're so fucking smart sometimes," Mike said.

Donetta sat up, her long hair dripping. "I hardly ever feel smart," she said. "I worry that you'll end up with somebody a lot smarter than me. And then when I do say something smart, you act like it makes you mad. So I just don't know what person you want me to be."

"Lie back down next to me," Mike said.

"No. You can't just make it all right like that."

He reached up and touched her smooth skin, which seemed to shine in the darkness. He pressed his hand against her back and felt her heart beating; touching her was like holding a bird, he thought, the way she seemed too small to be alive. And suddenly his face was wet. It just came from nowhere—more like rain than tears. He wanted to say that he was sorry for a hundred different things. He felt sorry for things that had nothing to do with her. He'd apologize to Mary Hise if he could. He'd say, My father didn't mean to do what he did.

"Mike?" she said. "What's wrong?"

He couldn't answer, even though he could hear how frightened she was. "Don't be mad at me," he said finally. "I can't stand it right now."

"Okay. It's all right. I'm not mad." She lay down and put her arms around him.

"I didn't mean for that to happen," Mike said. "I don't know what's wrong with me."

"It's okay," Donetta said. "I'm sorry."

She was saying what he should be saying to her. Things had gotten turned around, somehow—as if the responsibility lay with the darkness or the trees or the moonless sky. And whatever had happened to him was disappearing already, or going under the surface, like a rock thrown into water. He was all right again.

He and Donetta kissed. All around them in the black night were the sounds of insects and frogs. The noises just took over the night. It made Mike want to imitate them, leave being a person behind and be this thing that didn't require thought.

"I like the sounds," Donetta said. "I wish I could make them." She'd read his mind like that before. Or maybe he'd read hers, he thought. Maybe he had that backward.

They kissed more deeply. Donetta ran her fingers over his back, along his spine, from his neck down to the small of his back. Her breathing quickened with Mike's, though in the end they didn't let themselves have sex; the condoms were on shore, in the pocket of Mike's jeans. Donetta wouldn't take birth control pills. She'd feel slutty, she had told him; she'd feel like the kind of person who would fuck anybody. The only person she'd ever had sex with was Mike. The first time was just before her fifteenth birthday, in her empty house. She had said, afterward, "Isn't it strange that it hurts the first time? Do you think every good thing is like that?"

They swam back across the lake. Mike swam with her this time. He could see just flashes of her—a white arm, her face as she turned her head to breathe. She reached the shore before he did. He liked watching her—what he could see of her—walk naked out of the water. They didn't know where Josh and Pam were.

They dried off, dressed, and sat on the blanket, sharing a beer. They both heard Pam at the same moment—she cried out Josh's name. She and Josh were in the backseat of Josh's car.

"She's making a mistake," Donetta whispered to Mike.

He didn't answer. He was thinking that Pam's voice would come back to him in bed, that night, and the next time he and Donetta had sex. That was the difference between males and females. It was some ancient, inborn thing; therefore you didn't have to feel bad about it. It kept you separate, which made you strong enough to look out for the females and offspring. That's how they wrote about people in textbooks: males, females, offspring.

Still, he felt bad when Donetta took his hand.

"I wouldn't want anyone besides you to hear me," she whispered.

They got up and walked along the lake, away from the cars, until they couldn't hear anything human anymore.

TWELVE

Wylene Moseley returned home to Colorado by herself.

"We had her house watched," Tom said to them Thursday night, after dinner. "We knew she was back twenty minutes after she got there."

He had come over to the house this time without calling first—to catch them off guard, Mike thought, to catch *him* off guard, because it was Mike who was the target. Mike knew that, even if his mother didn't. His mother was the one to act too pleased to see Tom. She made him coffee and suggested they go outside on the patio, where it was cooler. It was dusk, and she lit citronella candles to keep the mosquitos away. Tom didn't sit down until she did.

"Wylene met Glenn at a bar," he told them. "A roadside place in the mountains. We knew about that bar earlier.

The bartender remembered Glenn and Wylene leaving together. He said he remembered because he used to go out with a friend of hers." Tom paused. "I figured he used to go out with Wylene. That's the kind of thing people lie about to policemen."

Carolyn smiled, but Mike didn't. His head had begun to hurt. He thought that it was starting to make him sick, seeing Tom DeWitt.

"Why did she trust him?" his mother said.

"They were close in age. He was polite. They liked the same music. She said that Glenn kept playing an old rock-and-roll song they both liked. Something about heaven. I can't remember the name."

Mike knew but kept still.

"It drives me crazy when I can't remember something," Tom said.

"Is it important?" Carolyn asked.

"No. But it's in my mind somewhere. Let me think for a minute." In the silence Mike watched Tom attentively survey the yard.

"I know it had *heaven* in the title," Tom said. "Heaven something or something heaven. Some word like *star.*"

"Mike, you know a lot about music," Carolyn said. "What song is he thinking of?"

They were both watching him; his headache grew worse. " 'Stairway to Heaven,' " he said finally.

"That's it," Tom said. He crossed his legs. Mike recognized his cowboy boots from the day he'd taken Mike to

Mary Hise's apartment. "How did you know it was that song in particular?" he asked Mike.

"It's famous."

"You and your dad must have the same taste in music," Tom said.

"They do," Carolyn said.

"We don't," Mike said.

"So he went home with her," Carolyn said then.

Tom looked from Mike to her. "Sorry," he said. "Yes. He followed her home."

"In what?" Carolyn asked.

"What kind of car did I say he had?"

"You didn't," Mike said.

"Oh. I thought I had. Well, it doesn't matter. It was barely running, and he used it as an excuse to stay with her for a few days. He told her that he was in trouble but couldn't say what kind. He said that he'd left his wife, and that he had a thirteen-year-old son." Tom paused there. He put his hand on the arm of Mike's chair. "He told her that you had leukemia."

Mike could feel, even without looking at her, how shocked his mother was.

"You mean that this made-up son did," Mike said. "If my father said it to begin with. You're only hearing it from her."

"I don't think she was making it up," Tom said. "It made too much of an impression on her. She'd had a sick child once, too."

"You don't know if that's true, either."

"We do," Tom told him. "We looked into it."

"What happened to her child?" Carolyn asked.

"He died."

The moon had come up, turning the grass and patio a milky color. Mike, his head hurting, wished that he were by himself, so that he could think about this without anybody watching him. He needed to think more clearly than he could now.

"There's not much else to tell," Tom said. "Glenn wanted to be driven as far away as she would take him. She said she'd drive him to Topeka, where her mother lived. They started out, then had the car trouble. They took back roads, ending up in Oklahoma, and she let him off at a bus station. She gave him money in exchange for the dog. She liked the dog. Then she drove up to Topeka for a visit. After that she drove straight home. No one stopped her, even though there was an all-points bulletin out."

"Did you tell her what Glenn did?" Carolyn asked.

"She said there must be more to it. That we needed to hear his side."

"Don't you ever think that?" Mike said. "Haven't you wondered about it even once?"

"No," Tom said. "I think I know his side." He took a drink of his coffee and set the cup on the table. "I think he meant to leave town with Mary, and that she didn't want to go."

"But you might be wrong," Mike said.

"Because he thought Mary still loved him," Carolyn said emotionally. "Because Mary hadn't quit yet."

"No," Tom said. "Because that's what he wanted to think."

Mike heard his mother exhale, or sigh. Her shoulders dropped as she leaned back in her chair.

"Do you remember my saying that Mary Hise had a boyfriend?" Tom asked.

"No," Carolyn said.

That was information Tom had given Mike the day they went to Mary Hise's apartment. Mike sat nervously and quietly, afraid that DeWitt would tell his mother that.

"We just found him in Idaho," Tom said. "He used to stop by Glenn's office when Mary was first working there. Glenn would tell her to stay away from him. Mary and the boyfriend fought a lot, apparently. Even Mary's neighbor said that. She said that the fights were pretty bad. You don't remember Glenn saying anything about him?"

"No," Carolyn said.

"He was here in May," Tom said. "He was sixty miles away the afternoon she was killed, but he and Mary had a date that night. The night she died. We just learned that. That was probably what the dress was for."

"That's a sad detail," Carolyn said.

"It is," Tom said, looking at Mike. "It makes you realize the things she'll never have. Children. A wedding and so forth. The boyfriend said he wanted to marry her."

"He was near Wheatley the same day she was killed?"

Mike said, hopeful in spite of himself. He was thinking that it was too big a coincidence not to matter. His father used to say that about mystery movies, that you could figure out who did it as soon as you saw a coincidence.

"We just learned that," Tom said a second time.

"And they fought a lot, right?" Mike said. "What about that? Dad might have been trying to protect her from him."

"Is that something your father would have done?"

Mike knew, then, that he'd let himself be tricked again.

"Yes," his mother said. "That would be just like him."

"Some men feel that very strongly," Tom said. "They exaggerate the harm somebody else could do. They underestimate the harm they themselves could do. They see themselves as heroes."

"How do you know how he sees himself?" Mike said.

"How do you think he saw himself that afternoon?" Tom asked.

"I don't know. I just said that you can never know."

"Take a guess."

"No," Mike said.

"Why not?"

"You know why not."

"I don't," Tom said. "I'm not a mind reader."

"Then don't ask *me* to be one," Mike said.

His mother stood up, suddenly, her chair scraping the concrete. "It doesn't matter," she said. "Nothing changes the fact that he killed her."

The conversation was over, and no one spoke. After a

From the Black Hills

minute Tom stood up as well. "One thing I feel bad about," he said. "I'm always bringing bad news."

"You can't help that," Carolyn said. "You're just keeping us informed."

"Maybe I shouldn't be."

"No," Carolyn told him. "I'd rather know than not know." She didn't consult or even glance at Mike.

Tom reached in his pocket for his car keys. "I'm heading up to my cabin tonight," he said. "I thought I'd stay there for a few days. I could use some time off." He looked down at Mike. "Do you like to fish?" he asked.

"No," Mike said.

"Well, you'd like it there, anyway. I'd bet on that."

Then he was gone. Mike didn't have enough energy to move, let alone go inside and find aspirin or go upstairs to lie down. And his mother was looking at him seriously, worriedly.

"That was a terrible thing for your father to say," she told him. "About the illness."

"It was just a story," Mike said. "We don't even know if he said it."

"I think he did. Couldn't you see that it bothered Tom to tell us?"

"You're not smart about him," Mike told her. "You don't see what he's up to."

"He wants to find your father," she said sternly. "I don't hold that against him."

"You don't hold anything against him," Mike said.

"What does that mean?"

Mike hesitated. "He wants us to see Dad the way that he does," he said then. "He thinks that we might know things."

"Like what? What could we possibly know?"

"Anything. He probably isn't sure what."

"You read too much into him," Carolyn said. "You're giving him intentions that he doesn't have."

"How do you know?"

"Because I listen to what he says, the same way you do." She stood there for a moment, watching Mike. Then, to his relief, she went into the house.

Mike blew out the candles and sat in the darkness, tired, hurting, and feeling ashamed, as if he'd invented his father's lie himself. It seemed to him that he was connected now to the death of somebody else, somebody he didn't even know— Wylene Moseley's child.

He heard a car pull up then and dreaded that it was De-Witt again, up to something else. But it was Josh, carrying a backpack, who walked up the driveway.

"Can I stay here tonight?" he asked Mike. He dropped his pack and slumped into a chair. "Duane King's been sending my mother flowers and shit. I said, 'You take him to court and then forgive him a week later? Are you crazy?'" In the house, a few minutes later, he said to Mike's mother, "Could you call her sometime and see if she's okay?" Then he went outside alone and sat in the grass under the crab-apple tree.

"Give him a little time out there," Carolyn said to Mike, who would have anyway, who knew Josh better than anyone did. He took two aspirin and watched his mother clean off the counters and the stove and sweep the floor. Finally he got out a Coke and took it out to Josh in the yard.

"Hey," Josh said. Mike sat under the tree with him. After a while Josh said, "I was so pissed at my mom that I felt like hitting her myself. How's that for fucked?"

"But you didn't do it," Mike said.

"I wanted to, though."

"Wanting doesn't count."

Josh drank his Coke as he and Mike watched old Clyde Pate, next door, come out to his back porch and sit down heavily on his porch swing. His wife had died the year before; Mike and his parents had gone to the funeral and brought food over afterward. "I feel so sorry for him," Mike's mother had said. "I feel sorry for anyone that alone."

Now Mike's mother was coming outside, crossing the lawn, bringing Mike and Josh each a bowl of ice cream. "I used to do this when you two were small," she said. "You probably don't remember."

"I do," Josh said.

She surprised Mike by sitting with them in the grass. She started talking about how soon it would be fall, and how they would be in college, leading their own independent lives. She told them about her own freshman year—how hard it was to leave home, yet what a relief it was to be away. "Some girls called their parents every night," she said. "I called once a week because I thought I should. I don't know what I thought would happen if I didn't."

"Why didn't you wait for them to call you?" Josh asked.

She seemed never to have thought of that. "Who knows?" she said. "Who knows why you do anything at that age?"

She picked up their empty bowls and crossed the yard to the kitchen—her old self again, Mike thought, though his mind was not on her but on his father. As the sky grew overcast and the night windy, he told Josh about Wylene Moseley, and about how his father had said he was sick. "Well, not me, exactly," Mike said. "This imaginary kid he made up, who was thirteen."

"Well, you were thirteen once," Josh said.

Mike's mother opened the back door and called to Josh. "Your mother's on the phone," she said. "Mr. King isn't there. She said to tell you that."

Josh went inside. Mike could see him standing in the middle of the kitchen, holding the receiver. Then Josh hung up and didn't come back out. Mike picked up his backpack and went inside. Upstairs, in the guest room, Josh was sitting alone in the dark.

"What's going on?" Mike said.

"Just more of the same shit. My mother thinks people are really sorry when they say they are. That's so fucking dense."

"Does she want you to come home?"

"I said I'd come by in the morning, before I left for Sheridan." He got up to look out the window. His mother's house was not far away; Mike could see the roof of it in the winter, when the trees were bare. "I wonder where old Glenn is right now," Josh said. "Like right at this instant."

"Some motel somewhere."

"Or somebody's house," Josh said. "Some other woman who believes his bullshit." He opened his backpack. "Can I smoke in here?"

Mike closed the door, got a window fan from the closet, and took one of Josh's cigarettes for himself.

"You shouldn't smoke with your illness," Josh said. "Plus, you're only thirteen."

"On the other hand, I already have cancer."

They laughed. After a while Mike went downstairs to smuggle a bottle of Jack Daniels out of the liquor cabinet. His mother was occupied with the news on television, though later she stopped outside the guest room on her way to bed.

"Don't stay up all night," she told them through the closed door.

"We won't," they said.

Mike sat on the bed, listening to Josh talk about Sheridan, Wyoming, and the Big Horn Mountains. "I backpacked up there one weekend," he told Mike. "I didn't want to come down. I thought, fuck everything."

"Fuck Pam," Mike said.

"Definitely fuck Pam."

Over the whir of the fan Mike could hear the wind rising again outside.

"The duplex we live in is at the edge of town," Josh said. "It's near the foot of the mountains. I can look out my window and see deer in the field behind us."

"I'm surprised they come so close."

"They have less to be afraid of there. You can't hunt that close to town."

"Still," Mike said.

Josh lit another cigarette. He was on the floor, leaning back against the closet. "Our duplex is kind of shabby," he told Mike. "The walls are thin. You can hear every sound."

"Like your dad with women?"

"No," Josh said. "Like him talking in his sleep. My mother's name and that."

"He hasn't met anybody else?"

"He has," Josh said, "but nobody he likes much. Nobody he wants to fuck, anyway." He tapped his cigarette ash into his hand. "I don't think he's trying very hard."

A tree branch brushed against the house. From where Mike was sitting he could see the brightness of the moon behind a veil of clouds. "The weather's changing," he said. "Maybe it won't be so hot tomorrow."

"Maybe not," Josh said. Mike handed him the Jack Daniels, and he shook his head. "I'm not feeling it. I only

get drunk when I'm trying not to." He put out his cigarette and got a book out of his backpack: *Sheep,* by Archer
Gilfillan.

"What's that about?" Mike asked. "I mean, what about
sheep?"

"He herded them," Josh said. "That's what he did for
eighteen years."

It was after midnight. Mike returned the bottle to the
liquor cabinet, made sure the front and back doors were
locked, and went up to his room. In bed, too drunk to
think clearly about either his father or Tom DeWitt, he
thought about Pam—how she'd looked that night at the
lake, and how she'd sounded in the backseat of Josh's
car. Mike could probably fuck her if he wanted to. She
wouldn't tell anyone. She wouldn't want to hurt Donetta.
She'd do it because she liked Mike; they liked each other.
They'd fuck and then they'd probably stop being friends.
But not because she wouldn't have liked it.

He fell asleep, then woke from a bad dream. He'd been
in an ambulance, too sick to move or talk. It had seemed so
real that Mike got out of bed now just to prove to himself
that he could. It was raining outside, and he looked across
the street at the Hylers' run-down house. It was haunted-
looking in the rain. It was a depressing thing to see. It
probably wasn't fixable even anymore. It took Mike three
hours to fall back asleep.

THIRTEEN

SCHOOL, suddenly, was only three weeks away. It had crept up on Mike, despite his mother's reminders. He'd stopped thinking about the future. His life had changed too much.

"I think I should stay home this fall," he said to his mother in the kitchen, early Sunday morning. "I'll work at the Schofields' and go to school next semester."

"Absolutely not," his mother said. "There's nothing worse than standing in one place, or going backwards."

"I couldn't go backwards if I tried."

But she refused to talk to him about it further. She left for church, and he went upstairs and stood in the doorway to the guest room, which had become a depository for items he would take to school, things his mother had been buying that Mike hadn't thought of even: a phone machine, a clock radio, a throw rug, a desk lamp. He'd been watching those things accumulate without feeling as if they were his. He closed the door now, so that he could walk down the hall without having to see them.

By the time his mother returned from church, he was down in the basement, cleaning the storm windows with vinegar and water. The temperature had dropped down to fifty during the night, the first sign of autumn. Cleaning and putting up the storm windows had been Mike's job since he was fourteen—his father had only supervised.

His mother came halfway down the rough basement steps in her dress and high heels. She sat down and watched him.

"You'll get dirty sitting there," he said.

"This dress is washable. Don't you want company?"

No, he thought. "Sure. Whatever."

"My students use that word," she told him. "I don't know where they get it from."

"Everybody says it."

"People your age, maybe," she said, no longer looking at Mike but at the boxes of his father's belongings, stacked in the right-hand corner of the basement. "I don't think this will come as a surprise," she told Mike. "But I want you to know. I've talked to a lawyer about divorcing your father."

Mike stopped working. "When?" he said.

"As soon as possible."

"I mean, when did you talk to a lawyer?"

"Two weeks ago."

Mike looked at the storm windows he hadn't washed yet—that probably wouldn't get washed, he thought, if it weren't for him. "Why do I have to learn about things after they happen?" he said. "Why can't you just tell me at the time?"

"Nothing's happened yet. And what should I do, ask your opinion? What kind of parent would I be if I put you in that position?"

"I'd just like to know what's going on," Mike said. "You don't have to get so pissed off."

"Don't use that phrase with me."

"Why not?"

"Because you should show more respect. Who do you think is taking care of you?"

"Nobody's making you do it."

"Who would be if I weren't?" his mother said.

"Me," Mike said. "I do it anyway." He put down his rag and walked past her up the steps. "I can't wait to get out of here," he shouted. He went out the kitchen door, slamming it behind him.

Outside, without his jacket or helmet, he got on his motorcycle and rode through town to Route 8, then out past the Schofield ranch in the direction of Badlands National Park. It was the only place he could think of to go, the only place that was far enough away and uninhabited enough to suit him. It was uninhabited by people, anyway. And it didn't cheer him up to know that he would be leaving

Wheatley in three weeks. Leaving didn't seem as if it would fix what was wrong.

It was a long ride. The wind was cool and the sun hot, and there was the lightness of not wearing a helmet. He rode through the Pine Ridge Indian Reservation, thinking that if he were in a car he could be listening to Indian music broadcast from Pine Ridge or Rosebud. Kids in town made fun of it—not Mike's friends, but assholes who didn't understand that you might want to hear something new or different, or that your own life might not be always what it was now.

Because you had to be ready for your life to change, even if you didn't want it to. The important thing, Mike thought, was being prepared for the next thing that happened—like his mother getting a divorce now that it no longer meant or solved anything, as opposed to a year ago, or six months ago, when it could have saved his father from killing Mary Hise. Mary could have quit work when she'd wanted to. She would not have had to see either one of Mike's parents again. She'd gotten caught between the two of them. Being unhappy made people do dangerous things.

Mike passed an old red Chevy driven at a crawl by an old man. And suddenly he just felt bleak, even though he could see, finally, the Badlands in the distance, the jagged edges of the jagged rocks, rising from the plains like dinosaurs.

He pulled off the road. He looked at the blank, blue sky, pulled back on the road in the opposite direction, and didn't stop until he got to the Schofield ranch.

· · ·

LEE-ANN was the only one home. As he walked up to the house, she came to the door in jeans and a sweater. "Neil's out at Ed's," she said. "He didn't say you were working today."

"I'm not here to work. I was just out riding."

She watched him from the doorway. It was hard for him to read her expression. "Come on in," she said.

Mike followed her into the living room, where the shades were drawn. There was an unfolded blanket on the couch.

"Where's Janna?" he asked.

"With Neil," she told him. "Sit down. Do you want a Coke?"

"No. I'm sorry I woke you up."

"It's okay." She sat down and looked at him closely. "What's wrong?" Out of nervousness he picked up the blanket and folded it. "You don't have to do that," she said. "You don't have to be so conscientious all the time."

Mike dropped it on the carpet.

"That's a small first step," she told him.

They sat there without speaking. The house was cold. The last time he'd been inside was when they'd kissed and he'd gotten sick, or whatever it was that had happened to him. He thought about saying, I'm leaving for college in three weeks. He thought about telling her that his mother was getting a divorce. Both things seemed wrong. The house had the same feeling it had had that afternoon in

May, when he'd come in alone and gone upstairs. He felt like he'd become less grown-up, over the summer, less sure of himself. He wanted to tell Lee-Ann what he'd done that day, so that she could see how unafraid he used to be. He reached for her hand.

"Listen," she said. "I'm glad to see you. But one minute it's like you're my son, and the next minute you're like my high school boyfriend or something. It's creepy."

"Thanks," Mike said. "That makes me feel like an asshole." He got up to leave and tripped over the blanket, falling against the couch. It was too clumsy not to be funny, and they both smiled.

"Sit down," Lee-Ann said. "It's my fault, too. It's probably more my fault than yours."

"There is no fault."

"I just want to be a friend to you," Lee-Ann told him. "I know you think you don't need it. But I'm a safe person for you."

"I don't know what you mean by safe," Mike said.

"I want what's best for you. And I'm not in a position to hurt you."

"I know. That's why it would be okay."

"It?" Lee-Ann said.

"You know," Mike said.

"I don't think that's what you need."

"How do you know what I need?"

"Well, I'm older than you."

"I forget that you're so old," Mike said. "You could be my grandmother, right?"

"Not quite."

"Listen," Mike said. "You don't feel the way you used to, I guess. That's okay. I mean, I can't change that."

Lee-Ann fingered the hem of her sweater. "I didn't say that exactly."

"So what are you saying?"

"It's complicated. I think one thing and feel another."

"So you should go with your feeling," Mike said.

"Why?"

"Because it's the same as mine. And because I'm leaving, and I won't see you for a long time."

"I've thought about that," Lee Ann said pensively.

The grandfather clock in the hallway chimed three times. In the stillness afterward, Mike moved close to her, put his arm around her, and kissed her. That was all he anticipated doing, to make up for last time. But when she didn't pull away, he kept his mouth on hers, and when he put his hand under her sweater she suddenly was responding to him as if she'd been waiting for this as long as he had. She was passionate and in a hurry. She interrupted their kissing only to take off her sweater and undo her bra as Mike pulled off his T-shirt. Her breasts were against his bare chest, and she moved his mouth down to her nipples, to one and then the other. "Take off your jeans," she whispered then, and took off her own while he removed his.

Then they were naked, Mike on top of her on the couch, almost inside of her, when she just stopped.

"Wait," she said. "I can't do this."

"Come on," Mike whispered. "It's okay."

"It's not okay."

"Lee-Ann," Mike said, but she was disentangling herself, then sitting up, looking for her clothes.

"I'm sorry," she told him. She put on her underwear and sweater and stood up to pull on her jeans. Mike still had an erection, and he dressed with his back to her. He stood in the middle of the dim living room, barefoot. He hadn't found his socks.

"I'm really sorry," Lee-Ann said. "You're never going to forgive me, are you?"

"Not anytime soon."

Mike sat in a chair, away from her. There was no way to get her body out of his mind. He watched her search under the couch for his socks. She handed them to him. "Are you okay?" she said.

"Why wouldn't I be?"

She sat down, too, her face still flushed. "When I was in the ninth grade," she told him, "in health class, they warned us about boys and their hormones. They said, 'Never put your hand in a boy's pocket.' I didn't understand why. I thought the boys would think we were trying to steal their money."

"You probably *were* trying to steal their money," Mike

said. He rested his head back against the chair and breathed deeply.

"I'm sorry," Lee-Ann said.

"I know. Stop saying that."

"I want to be good for you," she told him.

"You were doing a great job," Mike said.

"I mean without that. Because what I thought I could do, I can't."

"Okay."

She straightened out the couch cushions and folded the blanket. "It's not just Neil," she told him. "It's you, too."

"That's not a compliment," Mike said.

"You know what I mean. Your whole life got disrupted overnight. You've had this horrible summer."

"You were making it a lot better."

"Not in the long run, though. Even though it was really nice," she added, blushing, which made Mike feel somewhat okay. He tried to stop thinking about her breasts, and how she'd felt underneath him. He'd think about those things later, when he was alone.

They ended up in the kitchen, which was so familiar to Mike, and they sat at the table, looking out at the bright, cool afternoon. "I got pissed off at my mother today," Mike admitted then. "I just took off."

"Without your helmet," Lee-Ann said. "I noticed that. You should call her, tell her you're all right."

"Fuck her," Mike said, but then he got up and did it.

"I'm at the Schofields'," he told her, and, "Okay. I'll wear it next time. I'll see you in a while."

After that, more openly, he told Lee-Ann about his mother seeing a lawyer, and about Tom DeWitt trying to trip him up. "It's me he's always trying to get to. It's like he thinks I know something, like my father contacts me somehow. I can't trust him."

"You don't trust most people."

"I'd be stupid to."

"So you'd be stupid sometimes," Lee-Ann said. "So what?"

"I don't want people to see me that way."

"People are going to see you however they see you," she told him. "You have to separate people you can trust from people you can't. I'm in the first category," she told him. "No matter what."

It was after five. Outside the sun was illuminating the roof of the barn and the white fence along the road, and Lee-Ann began to make dinner. Mike set the table for her and helped her mash potatoes. Then he said, "I guess I should leave before Neil gets home."

They looked at each other.

"Either way is okay," Lee-Ann said. "He won't think anything of your being here." Her face flushed. "I'll re-member it, though," which gave Mike another erection.

He stayed a little longer, and before he left they said good-bye without touching. She waved to him, from the window, as he got on his bike. Riding down the driveway, he didn't feel anything extreme—just really relieved that he'd shown her what he could be like sexually. That was the important part. Otherwise he'd be feeling awful about himself.

LATE that night, he had a dream that was four months back in time. It was May, school was in session, and Mike had killed Kyle DeWitt in a wrestling match.

Awake, Mike had trouble remembering what month it was now. It took him a full few minutes to figure it out. The divorce thing had put him over the edge, he decided.

He focused on Lee-Ann. The places she wasn't perfect excited him most—the soft swelling of her stomach, her slightly fallen breasts. And he liked her white skin, which made her seem more naked than naked. Getting an erection made him forget his bad dream. What he liked was to imagine somebody and masturbate, so that how he felt wouldn't depend on anyone except himself.

FOURTEEN

I remind myself every morning that he's going," Donetta said to Mike's mother one afternoon three days before Mike was to leave for college. He was in his room, packing, and his mother and Donetta were on the stairs, carrying down boxes from the guest room. "If I keep reminding myself, I won't be so dramatic about it when he leaves."

"What do you mean?" Mike's mother asked.

"I'm not sure," Donetta said. "It's what my mother says I do."

Then they were downstairs, and outside, and Mike couldn't hear them anymore. From his window, he saw them standing in the driveway next to his new used pickup—a 1991 dark blue Ford Ranger Mike and his mother had bought the week before, with money Mike had saved and part of his mother's summer salary. He was taking his motorcycle, too, against his mother's wishes. They'd fought about it for a week. "I'm not going without it," Mike had said finally, that morning. "I don't care what you say," and he'd walked out of the room. They'd also fought about whether or not she should go with him to Brookings and help him settle in. She'd wanted to drive there with him, then fly back from Sioux Falls. "Are you kidding?" Mike had said, which had caused more trouble. Later he'd said, "I want to do this on my own." That was the kind of decision she respected.

A warm wind was coming in through Mike's window. Low clouds were moving east—toward Brookings, Mike thought, trying to make college seem more real. From his window he watched Donetta, in jeans and a tank top, lean over to tie her shoe. She had a pretty butt; that's all he was thinking, and suddenly he was looking at her through tears.

On the floor was a suitcase half filled with clothes, and another, empty one. Dust had gathered under his desk and bed; he hadn't cleaned his room lately, despite his mother asking him to. There was disorder in your life and then disorder in yourself; he'd read that somewhere. Anyway, it reminded him of his father, who probably had never in his life done the same thing in the same way two mornings in a row. He always threw a wrench in it somehow—like dropping his toothbrush in the toilet or knocking spices out of a cupboard in his effort to reach a coffee filter. "Why do you keep these shelves so crowded?" he'd yell at Mike's mother, and she'd say, "Grow up, Glenn." Then Mike's father would realize what a fool he looked like, and get in a worse mood. Meanwhile, Mike, sitting at the kitchen table, would keep eating his breakfast.

Outside now, Donetta was across the street, talking to Mrs. Hyler. The Hylers had eight cats. In the mornings Mrs. Hyler would be out on the porch, feeding them. Some were allowed in the house and some weren't; Donetta was always trying to learn which cats were the inside ones and which were the outside ones, and what determined which cats were which. "Do you think they can change categories?" Donetta would say to Mike. "Or do you think the outside cats can never be good enough to get inside?"

He watched her walk back to the street, turn around to wave good-bye, and come across the lawn, the wind lifting her hair. He listened to her running up the stairs. She had to leave, he knew; she was working the dinner shift at the diner.

"Mike?" she said, out of breath. "I have to get there early, to change into my uniform. I always hate for you to see me in it."

"You look good in it," he said. "You look good in everything."

"Do you really think that?" She put her arms around his neck. "Not that it matters, how you look. I know it doesn't."

She kissed him, and he pulled her close. But then they heard his mother come into the house. "I've got to go," Donetta told Mike. "I wish I didn't."

He went with her downstairs and walked her to her car; on the passenger seat of her Geo was a letter addressed to him at his dormitory address in Brookings. "You weren't supposed to see that," Donetta said. "It's so you'll get mail your first day there." Then she was in her car, driving off; he stood in the street until she rounded the corner. Then he walked across the yard, stooping under the low branches of the oak tree.

LATE in the afternoon, he and his mother got into his mother's car, with Mike driving, and left for Tom DeWitt's cabin in the Black Hills. Agreeing to go was Mike's way of compensating for the motorcycle argument. His mother was still angry at him. He could feel it in everything she said and did, even in the way she sat—too stiffly straight and close to the door. She had on new jeans and a light blue shirt and had taken a longer time than usual to get ready. She'd brought a dessert, covered with tinfoil, which she was holding on her lap.

"What's that for?" Mike asked.

"It's polite to bring something."

"What is it?"

"Coffee cake."

Mike stopped trying to make conversation. He took the more interesting way to Lead, through the National Forest, driving through Hill City and Silver City. He and Josh used to come up this way sometimes on Saturdays. They'd go to Deadwood to make fun of the tourists, or else they'd hang out in the cemetery above the town. Josh liked Wild Bill Hickok's grave. "Pard, we will meet again," Josh used to say at school, when he'd pass Mike in the hall. That was part of the sentence on Bill Hickok's gravestone, followed by GOODBYE, in a comma-shaped drawing.

Mike would walk through the highest, steepest section of the cemetery, where children were buried. It seemed spooky to him, how dangerous just being a child used to be. It would make your life a more intense thing, he'd think, as he stood there among the faded headstones, looking down at the strip-mined hills and the town screwed up with small casinos made to look like old-fashioned saloons. Sometimes you'd see a school bus go down that street, full of ordinary kids trying to grow up in a fucked-up place.

"Don't forget to give me whatever clothes you need washed," Mike's mother said. "I don't want to be doing laundry at the last minute."

He nodded, hardly listening.

"Make a list of things you haven't done yet," she told him. "That's the only way you'll remember."

As they got closer, she read him directions: left near a ranger station, then past a log cabin. The sun was getting low, and they were on a winding road with pines on one side and Elk Creek on the other. "Turn here," his mother said at a dirt road that led uphill. A quarter of a mile through the woods was a small frame house with Tom DeWitt's car parked next to it. The door opened, and he came outside.

"I'm sorry we didn't get here earlier," Carolyn said. "We've been getting Mike ready for school."

"That sounds like I'm in the first grade," Mike said.

"No, it doesn't." She turned her back on him, and he heard the way she sucked in her breath. Give it up, Mike wanted to say to her. Stop being an asshole. He walked inside behind her.

"I can show you around in under two minutes," Tom said, and walked them through the main room, which had a rustic kitchen at one end and a living room at the other, with a wood burner in the middle. The walls were pine, stained dark. Down the hall was a small bathroom and bedroom, the bed made up with a red wool blanket. Also in the bedroom were a phone, an answering machine, and a tiny television. "I don't completely rough it," he said, "as you can see."

"When you find my dad," Mike told him, "you'll be able to see yourself on television."

"Why would you say something like that?" his mother said.

"Look," Tom said. "If I wanted a movie career, I'd go to Hollywood. It's not like I haven't had offers." When neither Mike nor Carolyn laughed, he said, "I'm kidding. It's a joke."

He led them into the living room and brought them beers. "I assume it's all right for Mike to have one?" he asked, and handed it to Mike before his mother had a chance to answer.

"I want to look around outside," Mike said abruptly. He walked out on the porch, then down past the cars into the cool, dark shadows of the pines. Behind him, he heard the door open.

"Mike?" his mother said.

He didn't speak or move. After a minute she went inside, and he walked down the hill and along Elk Creek, which was wide and shallow, though its banks were steep. He stood in the gathering dusk, drinking the beer he didn't want much, tired of his mother, tired of whatever attempts Tom DeWitt would make tonight to manipulate him or whatever it was he always did. His mother was a fool where DeWitt was concerned. Mike's father used to say, "Your mother wants to believe that people are better than they are," and he also had been right about how controlling she was, and what it did to you after a while.

Mike watched the creek for muskrats or beaver. The temperature was lower here, as it always was in the Hills. Before long, Mike thought, there would be the first frost— maybe not right here but farther south and higher up, toward Harney Peak. It would snow there then, and you could go from fall to winter just by driving out of Wheatley up to Hill City. It wasn't far, though the roads were twisting and narrow, and coming back down into Wheatley you'd have long views again of long grass, which would seem almost liquid, put in motion by the wind blowing through them.

Those were just his thoughts, and all at once he was overcome with homesickness and uncertainty. He felt lost somehow, even from himself, and it was hard for him to take a breath. The ground under him seemed unsubstantial, and the way he felt was nothing he could find words for; maybe it was like dying, he thought, and for a second he almost believed that he was, though he didn't know of what, or what had made it happen. It was like being caught high in the air, like in a flying dream, except that you couldn't fly. You couldn't even fall. And there were no stars or planets above you, or earth beneath you.

Then, as suddenly as the fears had come, they faded, and within a few minutes Mike found himself paying attention again to the creek, and to the night sounds in the growing darkness. The tightness inside him went away. It went below ground, somehow. Mike stood in the dusk, listening to the creek, and didn't turn around and walk back until he started feeling angry again—at his mother, particularly, for causing him to feel so bad.

When he entered the house, Tom said, "There's more beer in the refrigerator. Help yourself."

"One is plenty," Carolyn said, which was the only reason Mike helped himself to a second one. He stood near the wood burner, while his mother and Tom DeWitt sat at opposite ends of the couch.

"Are you ready for school to start?" Tom asked Carolyn.

"Yes," she said at first. Then, "I don't know. I suppose so."

"You teachers should get paid more," he said. "I don't know how you do it, spending every day with kids who'd rather be someplace else."

"Some of the students want to be there," Carolyn said.

"No, they don't," Mike said. "Not in a class, anyway."

"So now I'm a bad teacher."

"He didn't say that," Tom said.

Carolyn put down her beer and stood up. "Excuse me," she said, and walked down the dark hall to the bathroom.

"You don't have to defend me," Mike said to Tom.

"Sit down."

"Why?"

"Because it hurts my neck to look up. And I want to tell you something." He got a card out of his pocket and handed it to Mike. There were three phone numbers on it. "When your father contacts you at school," he said, "I want you to call me."

Mike's head began to hurt. "How do you know he will?" he said.

"I don't. I just think it's going to happen."

"Then where is he now?" Mike said.

"I'm not sure."

The bathroom door opened, and Tom stood up when Carolyn walked into the room. "I spoke out of turn," he told her. "I'm sorry. I have a tendency to do that."

"That makes two of us," she said. She turned to Mike. "I didn't mean to jump on you, either."

Mike was too distracted to reply. He was thinking about

how he'd get rid of Tom's card later, throwing it away someplace his mother wouldn't find it. Meanwhile, he put it in his pocket.

THEY had dinner at the small kitchen table. Tom had made chili, which Carolyn made a fuss over. "Don't give me too much credit," he told her. "It's mostly out of a can. But I'm glad you like it."

He was smiling at her, helping her to more, and for the first time Mike thought that Tom seemed less sure of himself—maybe even nervous. He did most of the talking. He told them about seeing a mountain lion a few weeks earlier, and about how many more coyotes there were around than people thought, and how much more Mike's mother must know about science than he did, given that she taught biology. Then the phone rang, and he went into the bedroom to answer it.

"That's why he keeps it in the bedroom," Mike said to his mother. "So that he can talk in private."

"Don't be paranoid. How much company do you think he gets?"

"What I'm saying is, he's always working. Even when you think he's not."

"Mike," his mother said hesitantly. "Are you jealous that he seems to like me?"

No, he started to say. Then he realized how useless it could be to tell the truth, to think that you weren't alone, on your own, in every situation. "Maybe I am," he told her. "Maybe that's right."

She smiled at him for the first time in a week. "That's only natural," she said gently.

When Tom DeWitt came back to the table, they finished their chili. They ate the coffee cake.

FIFTEEN

$\mathbf{M}$ IKE wasn't sure where to take Donetta for their last night together. If they went to Crow Lake, she'd know he wanted to have sex with her. If he didn't take her there, she might think he didn't care about having sex with her. He was overly preoccupied with it, and with other things as well, especially saying good-bye to Lee-Ann. He wanted to make exactly the right impression—confident but not arrogant, easygoing but not immature. Whatever he was like today would be what she would remember, he thought. He didn't always realize that there was latitude with people, built-up stock, that most people didn't think you were only what you were on any one day.

He drove to the Schofields' early in the morning, the day before he was to leave. The sun had just risen, and there were antelope in the low hills above the Schofields' property. Near the barn, next to the old lean-to Neil had bought, Neil and Ed were at work on a new project: an old jailhouse they had bought and moved there from Montana. "So we can arrest each other," Neil joked to Mike. Then he said, "Shit," and hit himself in the forehead.

"It's okay," Mike said. "I wish everybody would forget about it like that."

Neil and Ed admired his new truck—it was the first time they had seen it—and gave him advice about college.

"Wear condoms," Ed said.

"Only go to class if there's nothing better to do," Neil told him. "I mean it. Have fun sometimes." He put an arm over Mike's shoulders. "Say good-bye to Lee-Ann, or she'll never forgive you. She has something for you."

Lee-Ann was waiting for him at the open kitchen door. Behind her, Janna was in her high chair, eating Cheerios; Mike sat next to her. On the table in front of him were five stamped envelopes, addressed to Lee-Ann. "So you won't have an excuse not to write," she told him. She was barefoot, dressed in shorts and a loose shirt, her soft hair uncombed. She handed him a greeting card, which said, "Good luck in your new life from your friends in your old life." Inside was a check for five hundred dollars.

"I can't take this," Mike said.

"Force yourself. It's for extras, like movies and pizza. Or maybe a trip home some weekend." She got coffee for herself and Mike. "Are you excited about going?" she asked him. "Or are you nervous?"

"Neither. It's just school."

"Four hundred miles away, though."

"It's only a day's drive."

Lee-Ann looked at him thoughtfully.

"What?" Mike said.

"Going away to college is a big deal," she told him.

"Not to me."

"Well, it should be," Lee-Ann said.

"It doesn't seem important," Mike said, "compared to everything else."

"You have to make it important."

"I'd rather stay here," Mike said, and when Lee-Ann looked startled, he explained, "I mean in Wheatley."

They sat silently in the sunny kitchen, Janna smiling between them. Mike looked at the white-tiled floor and the shiny appliances, and the hallway leading to the living room. He could see in his mind exactly how Lee-Ann had looked, naked, on the couch, but equally vivid was the afternoon in the barn when he'd held her. That had grown in significance. He knew that neither of those things would happen again.

"It's going to be lonely, not seeing you," Lee-Ann said.

"I know. It will be for me, too." Mike turned to Janna so that Lee-Ann couldn't see how sad he was. "What about you?" he said. "Are you going to miss me?" Janna took a Cheerio out of her mouth and offered it to Mike. "That's what I thought," he said.

Before he left, he and Lee-Ann hugged, as friends, without kissing and without intensity, and Mike felt fine until Lee-Ann hugged him longer than he'd expected her to. He didn't know why that affected him so strongly, why that, more than anything else, seemed to divide his life in Wheatley so definitively and permanently from the life he would have from tomorrow on.

"You have to come see us whenever you're home," Lee-Ann said, and Mike thought: I feel like I'm never going to come back home.

"You know I will," he said.

She walked him outside into the warm sun. Then he was on his own, waving to Neil and Ed from a distance, starting his truck, and heading down the long driveway. It was when he got to Route 8 that he knew he couldn't face Wheatley. He needed to be alone someplace.

He drove to Hot Springs, then up into the Black Hills all the way to Custer. His windows were down. The road was crisscrossed with strips of sun and shadow, and the hills were green and dark with pines. He felt better now that he was alone in his truck, concentrating on driving.

Still, returning later to Wheatley, he could not think about Lee-Ann Schofield. It was like having a toothache, or a cut too tender to touch. She got to him somehow. She knew him too well. She didn't allow him to keep his defenses up.

·   ·   ·

LATER in the day he finished packing: his books, his computer, his school supplies. He mowed the yard one last time and had a steak supper with his mother in the dining room—a celebratory supper, she said. "We're going to leave the past behind," she told him. "That's where it belongs, doesn't it? The past belongs in the past."

"I guess so," Mike said. He wasn't hungry, but he ate to please her.

"If Tom comes by with new information," his mother said to him, "I'll let you know only if it's something significant. I don't want you distracted from school."

"He'll probably let me know himself," Mike said, to see if she knew more than he thought she did.

"Of course he won't. He wouldn't do that without telling me first."

Mike said nothing. On the wall above where she sat was a square blank space where a picture of their family used to hang: Mike at age ten, with his parents standing behind him. He hadn't remembered his mother taking it down. He was noticing only now that it was gone.

His mother cleared the table and brought in, as a surprise, a chocolate bakery cake with GOOD LUCK, MIKE written on it. Mike, cutting them each a big piece, tried to act happy.

HE drove through Wheatley just as the streetlights were coming on. It was a windy night, and the streets were empty except for a group of high school kids fooling around in the Taco John parking lot. Mike went out of his way not to drive past his father's office. He took a route past the hardware store and the community college, and as he turned onto Flat Rock Road the moon, rising behind him over town, looked impossibly big.

When he pulled into Donetta's driveway, he saw that the front door was wide open. Moreover, there was Cory Burris, walking up to it with a baby goat in his arms.

"It's okay," Cory called out. "She's just unconscious. She'll come to in a few hours."

"Not in this house she won't," Mrs. Rush said. Mike could see a tearful Margo behind her.

"Why would somebody give Wild Turkey to a baby?" Cory asked Mike. "Party or no party?"

"I have no idea," Mike said.

"Donetta's in the kitchen," Mrs. Rush told him, step-ping aside to let Mike in, and Cory ran in right behind him. He lay the goat down in a cardboard box that Donetta was lining with towels. He and Margo hovered over it.

"She doesn't look good," Margo said.

"That's because she's dead," Mrs. Rush said from the front hall.

"Being negative is harmful," Margo told her mother. "How many times has Pastor Kelly said that?"

"Don't throw Pastor Kelly at me," Mrs. Rush said. "Dead

is dead. Furthermore, the goat isn't my fault. I wouldn't attend a party where people gave liquor to an animal."

"I was just passing by," Cory said defensively.

Next to Mike, Donetta knelt down, patted the goat's head, and burst into tears.

"For Pete's sake," Mrs. Rush said. She came into the room and put her hands on Donetta's shoulders. "Just calm down," she whispered. "Don't be like this on Mike's last night home."

IT was almost nine by the time they left for Crow Lake. It was Donetta's idea to go there. "I want to go someplace that seems like ours," she told him. "Someplace really private."

"We don't have to have sex," Mike said. "It's not like that's the only reason I see you."

Donetta had been sitting close to him, but she moved over now and looked out her window. Then she said, "That's not the only reason you *see* me? That's an egotistical thing to say. It's like you're doing me a favor. Or else it's like you see me and then who else do you see? Who else *will* you see?" she asked, correcting herself. Before Mike had a chance to answer, Donetta said, "I told myself I wouldn't do this. Pastor Kelly said it was self-destructive."

"You saw Pastor Kelly?"

"Just once," Donetta explained. "I went by myself. I didn't tell anyone."

"Why didn't you just talk to me?"

"Because it was about you," Donetta said. "It was about you with me, anyway."

"I guess you don't trust me very much," Mike said indignantly.

"I know," Donetta said. "That's what I talked to him about."

Mike's face reddened. He couldn't think of a response. After a minute he reached for her hand and held it as he drove. She didn't pull it away.

HE parked where they always did, a little distance from the lake, out of sight of the road. Donetta rolled down her window. In the darkness came the sound of wind through the trees. Mike waited for Donetta to say something. When she didn't, he touched her white dress. "Is this new?" he asked awkwardly. She nodded. "I like it," he told her. "It looks good on you."

"I ordered it from a catalogue. I got it for tonight." She turned her face toward the open window. "That's the kind of lovesick thing I do for you."

"That's not lovesick," Mike said. "I don't even know what that means."

"It's what you always say about me. Not that word, exactly, but that I think about you too much. Which is like saying, 'You think about me more than I think about you.' "

"Well, I was wrong," Mike said.

She got out of the car and walked down the dark path to the edge of the water. There was enough moonlight for Mike to see her, but he couldn't tell if she was crying. He felt depressed and defeated. He didn't know, anymore, what she thought, or how he came across to anyone.

He walked down to the water and stood beside her. "I'm not as bad as you think," he said.

"What does that mean? Like, 'I'm bad, but I could be worse'? Well, so could everybody." She crossed her arms. "I'm trying not to be stupid."

"You don't have to try. You're not."

"Stupid is when you love the wrong person," Donetta said.

He stepped back clumsily, and when Donetta saw his face she moved close to him. "I shouldn't have said that," she whispered. "I should have used different words." She put her arms around him. A car drove up on the other side of the lake, and they heard people get out. One of them said, "The water's cold."

"I've fucked up this night," Donetta said.

"No, you haven't."

"I think it started with the goat. I felt okay until then."

They walked back to the truck, holding hands. Mike opened the door for her, and they sat together on the wide front seat. The windows were open to the sounds of frogs and cicadas, wind and water. For Mike everything about Donetta suddenly seemed important—how she felt, what she thought, how this night would seem to her tomorrow.

"I wish I didn't have to go," he said.

"Do you really feel that way?"

"Yes."

She kissed him, and for a while that was all they did. Now that he was leaving so soon, he wasn't in a hurry. He wanted to delay time instead of speeding it up. Donetta was wearing only her dress and sandals, and she took them off while Mike was still dressed. It aroused him to see her naked when he wasn't, to see her smooth skin against the rough fabric of the seat. She unbuttoned his shirt as he undid his belt. She watched him as he took off his jeans.

They had sex on the front seat, Mike trying not to put too much weight on her. He held himself over her carefully and, after he had an orgasm, stayed inside her as long as he could. He looked down at her face and shoulders, aware as always of how small she was. And all at once he realized that if anyone was likely to hurt her, it would be him. Not physically—nothing like what his father had done—but in terms of her feelings, which was exactly what she'd been saying earlier.

Afterward he watched her put on her dress, reach for her purse, and brush her hair. He got out of the truck and looked at the dark woods, beyond which were fields; beyond the fields were the Black Hills, which he'd seen, in the distance, practically every day of his life. Beginning tomorrow he'd see something else—it didn't matter what. It wouldn't be as good or mean as much. It wouldn't make him remember specific moments in his life, such as this one. It wouldn't be home to him.

"What are you thinking about?" Donetta asked.

"You," he said, shivering as he said it.

ON the way home he made her put on her seat belt. "You should always wear it," he told her. "It should be the first thing you do when you get in the car."

"What about you, with your motorcycle helmet?" she said. "You never want to wear it."

"I do, though."

"Not all the time."

"Then I should. I will," he said. "Anyway, you have to be careful, especially because your car's so small. It's not that safe."

"Does that mean you love me?" Donetta asked.

"Yes." He took her hand and held it tightly.

After they turned onto Flat Rock Road, they both, at the same moment, spoke of the goat. Donetta said, "I hope the goat's alive," and Mike said, "The goat might be okay. Cory might have been right."

"He hardly ever is, though," Donetta said.

Mike pulled into her driveway. The house was dark except for the outside porch light and a light on in Donetta's room. Donetta got a tape cassette out of her purse and put it in his hand.

"I made this for you," she told him. "Don't listen to it until tomorrow, when you're on the highway. You have to promise."

"I promise," he said.

They embraced, her wet face against his shirt. "I'll still be in South Dakota," he told her. "I'll just be at the other end of it." He'd intended it to be funny, but it didn't sound funny. He didn't feel humorous. When Donetta moved in order to reach for a Kleenex, he didn't want to let her go.

It was one in the morning when he walked her up to the door. "If you fall in love with somebody," Donetta said, "tell me. Don't make me figure it out."

"I won't."

"Unless it's with me," she said, so softly that he didn't catch the words until she'd opened the door and gone inside. He stood there a minute, under the yellow porch light. Moths fluttered above his head, and from inside the house he heard Donetta's mother call her name.

He opened the door to his truck and could smell her perfume. He backed down the driveway, and on Flat Rock Road, before it curved to the west, he pulled over and got out. He stood on the shoulder of the road, looking back at her house. It was small from this distance, one of three with lights burning. There weren't all that many houses, anyway, and they were far apart, like stars, he thought, in what was mostly dark and vacant space. He knew which light was the light in Donetta's bedroom, and when it went out was when he really understood that he was leaving.

He drove home listening to the tape Donetta had made for him. The first thing on the cassette was her voice. "It's three o'clock in the morning," she said. "I can't sleep, I can't dream, and I can't stop thinking of you."

The first song was "Miss You," by the Rolling Stones.

SIXTEEN

S AYING good-bye to his mother was easier.

She got him up at seven and helped him finish loading his truck; she made him waffles as well as a lunch to take with him. She was dressed for church in a skirt so new it had a price tag hanging from it.

"You might want to take that part off," Mike told her, and she laughed and got out scissors.

"Do you think you'll miss this house?" she asked at breakfast. "It's the only place you've ever lived."

"Maybe," Mike said. He didn't add that he'd miss her.

"Did you sleep all right?" she asked then.

"Yes," he said, though he hadn't. He'd dreamed that somebody his own age was trying to run him down with a truck. Awake, then, he'd become nervous about ordinary sounds: the refrigerator starting up, downstairs; a car speeding down the street. By the time he had fallen back asleep, it was almost dawn.

"I'm going to keep tutoring at the college," his mother told him. "I'm helping Jim Reynolds on Tuesday nights. In fact," she added, "I'll probably see him at church this morning."

"He goes to Saint Ann's?"

"He just joined."

"Well, good for him," Mike said.

"Are you being sarcastic?" his mother asked. When he didn't answer she said, "Never mind. You say what you want." She drank her coffee. "Don't ever skip breakfast," she told him. "You can't think on an empty stomach."

"Who said I was going to think?" Mike said, and his mother smiled. It was probably the nicest moment between them all summer.

She walked out with him into the warm, sunless morning. They spoke for a few minutes, said their good-byes; soon after that he was heading east—driving away from his house, from Wheatley, and from the Black Hills. In front of him the sun emerged briefly, then withdrew into a bank of clouds.

PART II

BROOKINGS

SEVENTEEN

IT was drizzling by the time Mike reached Brookings and found his dormitory, Hansen Hall. When he'd come to campus in October, with his parents, he hadn't known where he would live. He'd pictured one of the older, red-brick dorms in the center of campus. But Hansen Hall was at the western edge of the university, on Eleventh Street. It was a newer building, a rectangle four stories high, with a dimly lit lobby in the middle that separated the west wing from the east wing. Males west and females east, the desk clerk told him; she was an older student—older than Mike, anyway—studying an economics textbook. "Is there an elevator?" Mike asked. His room was on the fourth floor.

"No," she said, smiling briefly. She returned to her book.

Mike's room was at the end of a long, plain hall and faced the street. The door was open. A tall, brown-haired boy was sitting next to the window, in front of a computer. "Raymond Nelson," he said, getting up to shake Mike's hand. He had a thin face and wore glasses. His limp hair was collar-length.

"Hi," Mike said, looking at the beds, one on each side, raised up on iron posts more than five feet off the floor. There were rungs at each end.

"It's so that we can use the space underneath," Raymond told him. That was how small the room was. At the foot of each bed was a desk, and above each desk were three small shelves. "I'm on the left side," Raymond said. "Though I can switch if you want."

"No. That's okay," Mike said. "How long have you been here?"

"Since Friday." He was already engrossed again at the computer. Mike could see some kind of drawing on the screen. Raymond's computer was more sophisticated than his was.

Mike went downstairs and unloaded his truck, carrying suitcases and boxes into the lobby. His hair and denim jacket were wet by the time he finished. A boy who'd come down to watch television helped Mike carry things up the four flights of stairs. "Thanks," Mike said.

"No problem."

Raymond looked up, surprised, when Mike came back in, lugging suitcases. "Sorry," he said. "I kind of got into this thing I'm doing."

"What is it?"

"High-tech space warfare." He helped Mike bring in the remaining items and watched him unpack the first box: a striped rug, tan curtains, and a phone machine. "Wow," he said. "You thought of all that stuff?"

"My mom did. She said that if you already had any of it, I could just bring mine back home."

"I don't," Raymond said. He took the rug from Mike and put it on the bare floor, under the beds. "Homey," he said. At first Mike thought he was kidding. But Raymond watched with a lot of interest as Mike unpacked a microwave.

"I have money for a small refrigerator, too," Mike said, "in case you don't have one."

"Shit," Raymond said. "I don't. That's great."

"She memorized every word of everything the school sent me," Mike told him.

"That's lucky."

"That's one way to look at it."

"What's another?" Raymond asked. He was serious.

"I don't know," Mike said. "I was just talking."

For the next two hours he unpacked, putting his clothes in the small dresser and closet at the head of his bed. From down the hall he could hear a television; Raymond didn't have one, and Mike's mother hadn't wanted Mike to have one. Mike hadn't argued with her; he'd worried about hearing or seeing something about his father on the news. It was bad enough that he had brought a radio.

During the seven-hour drive to Brookings he had

planned what he'd say to people who recognized his last name: "He's a relative I hardly knew," or, to people who somehow knew more: "My mother's divorcing him." Mike worried about teachers who might know but not say anything. He hated for anyone to know more about him than he knew they did. Thoughts along those lines had occupied him for the whole seven hours.

"Are you hungry?" Raymond asked, after Mike had set up his computer. "We could walk to Mad Jack's. It's not far."

"Okay," Mike said. He had forgotten that he hadn't eaten.

They went downstairs and through the lobby, empty now except for two girls watching an old black-and-white movie on television. "Don't you wish guys dressed up like that now?" one of the girls said. "And took us dancing?"

Outside the rain had stopped. The night was warm, and so muggy that halos of mist surrounded the streetlights. "It's pretty humid here," Mike said.

"You're West River," Raymond said. "I thought you'd show up in a cowboy hat." West River, Mike knew, meant that you lived west of the Missouri River, and that you spent more time with cows and horses than with people.

"I left it home with my spurs."

Raymond laughed. "A lot of people didn't."

Mad Jack's, across the street from campus, was crowded and noisy. In a back corner was a large group of students who seemed to be getting together for the first time that semester. They were informal and cheerful. At another table were three scornful-looking long-haired guys.

Mike and Raymond sat at a table next to the window and ordered a pizza. Beyond their reflection in the glass, Mike could see the bell tower across the street, lit up from below. It was four or five times as high as the big elm trees around it.

"I've only gotten lost once," Raymond said. "The campus is not that big." He had weak brown eyes and pale bad skin. "I wanted to go to school out of state," he told Mike. "I was interested in an engineering program at Purdue University. Dad said, 'There's nothing in Indiana you won't find here.' "

"Except Hoosiers," Mike said.

"That's good," Raymond said. "I wish I'd said that."

Mike started to ask about his father—if he was some kind of engineer, himself, up in Aberdeen. But he caught himself. He needed to stay focused on college, or the future, so that Raymond—or anyone Mike talked to—wouldn't ask him about his own family and past. "Isn't there some kind of meeting Dr. Boyd is having tomorrow?" he asked instead. Dr. Boyd was the head of the honors program, whom Mike and his parents had met the previous fall.

Raymond nodded. "At ten," he told Mike. "Maybe we can catch breakfast beforehand."

They were finishing their pizza when the group of students in the corner got up to leave. At another table, a pretty, blond-haired girl looked over and smiled at Mike; her smile died when she looked at Raymond. Raymond wasn't paying attention. He'd taken a pencil out of his shirt pocket and was drawing what looked like a space station on his napkin.

"I get these ideas sometimes," he said to Mike. "Suddenly I'll just have a solution to a problem." He folded the napkin and put it in his pocket. On the short walk back to Hansen Hall, he took it out once and looked at it.

In their room the phone machine was flashing. There was a message from Mike's mother: "Did you forget to call when you got in?"

Mike called her back. "Sorry," he said. "Raymond and I went out to eat."

"What is he like?"

"Okay," Mike said. "You know." Raymond was in the room, working at his desk again.

"Where did you eat?"

"Mad Jack's. A pizza place," Mike said. He imagined her shaking her head. "It's just a few blocks away."

"So the drive was all right? I was afraid you'd run into rain."

"It was drizzling when I got here," he told her.

"Well, I'm glad you had a safe trip." She was silent for a moment. "The house feels a little lonely," she said then, "a little too big. But I'll survive it. I'll get used to it."

"I told you I'd stay home," Mike said.

"Don't be silly. I'll be fine. You take care of yourself. Get settled in and buy your books, and I'll talk to you later in the week. Call me if you need anything."

"I will." Mike stayed where he was after he hung up, looking at the concrete-block walls and the ugly, industrial-looking beds. Even the view from the window was poor: just the wide, flat streets and a row of small houses, probably rented to students.

Mike picked up the phone to call Donetta but put it back down. Because she would say that she missed him, and what would Mike say—that what he missed were the fields on either side of Route 8, as he rode out to the Schofields'? Or the antelope you could see early in the morning or just before dusk? He was missing things more than people. He missed how things made him feel.

Though it wasn't even eleven o'clock, he got up into bed, which was narrower and less comfortable than his bed at home. The room was dark except for Raymond's desk lamp, a small circle of light shining down on the keyboard.

Mike listened to the rain start again and to Raymond at his computer. He wasn't used to having somebody in the room with him. He'd always slept alone except for the nights, in childhood, when Josh had slept over. Mike hadn't liked it even then. As he'd gotten older he'd tried to hide that fact about himself, because on TV, weirdos were always described as antisocial, or loners. They turned into serial killers when they grew up.

Raymond turned off his computer, left the room for a few minutes, and came back in. He got into bed.

"Did you finish what you were doing?" Mike asked him.

"Almost. I thought you were asleep."

"Not yet."

"That was your mom who called before?"

"I was supposed to call when I got here," Mike said.

"I do E-mail. It's easier."

"Your parents have a hookup at home?"

"Dad does," Raymond said. Then, "It's not parents, exactly. I have a stepmother and a stepbrother. My mother died four years ago."

"Oh," Mike said.

"She had cancer."

Mike didn't speak, afraid that anything he said wouldn't sound serious or sincere enough.

"You can get E-mail here easily. I can show you."

"Thanks."

After a small pause, Raymond said, "People get freaked out when you say your mother's dead. I just like to say it and get it over with."

"I know," Mike said. "I mean, I don't know, but I know what you mean." He wished he could say: I know because my father's dead, so that whatever his father had done might be erased. Finally he said, "It doesn't freak me out. I just think it's sad."

"Okay."

Only a few minutes passed before Mike could tell, by Raymond's breathing, that he was asleep. Mike never fell asleep that quickly, not since he'd been eleven or twelve. He'd always thought of it as a sexual thing, as if puberty had gotten in the way of sleep. Nights were when you thought about girls and sex. He got an erection now, thinking about the girl at Mad Jack's who had smiled at him. She'd been wearing a tight little top and no bra. He'd caught her looking at him a few more times. But he had trouble now keeping her in his head. Other things intruded—worries about school, thoughts about home—and his erection disappeared.

The problem was being in a new place, in a new phase of his life, while feeling, somehow, that he hadn't come to terms with the old phase. He couldn't catch up with the things that had happened to him. Worse, there was an acceleration to it now, sending him at a faster rate further and further behind.

He closed his eyes and tried to lie exactly in the center of the bed, as if he were in a boat in danger of capsizing.

EIGHTEEN

THERE were 1,294 freshmen at South Dakota State, including Mike. There were something like 5,000 undergraduates in all. Nonetheless, late Friday afternoon in the University Union, he almost ran into a girl he knew from high school. He managed to escape into a rest room before she saw him.

Afterward he went to Hansen Hall to pick up his mail—a letter from his mother and one from Donetta—and retreated to the privacy of McCrory Gardens, on the opposite side of campus. He found a bench half hidden by dogwood trees.

He opened Donetta's letter first. He'd already received two from her, including the letter he'd seen sealed, in her car, before he left for school. The one he opened now said,

"Guess what? The goat *was* alive, and she and Sophie are be-coming friends. They sleep together in the cardboard box."

Toward the end of the letter she wrote, "You know what I have on right now? A white T-shirt you can almost see through. I want to take it off for you and do things you've never done with anyone else and never will." That excited him, then upset him a moment later. It implied that he'd been unfaithful in the past and predicted that he'd be un-faithful in the future. Why would she want to think of him that way?

Also in the envelope was a little watercolor she'd done: a painting of the cottonwood tree whose limbs bent down low over Lame Johnny Creek. In the bottom right-hand corner were her uncapitalized initials: *dsr.* What was the *s* for? Mike knew but couldn't remember. He went through every *S* name he could think of. He repeated "Donetta something Rush" to himself over and over again. Finally, giving up, just looking at red poppies planted along the gravel path, the name Senn came into his head—a family name on her mother's side. Donetta Senn Rush. He felt re-lieved to remember it, as if he were afraid of losing his memory or even his mind.

His mother's letter was short. She'd run into Lee-Ann Schofield, who'd said to tell Mike that Janna kept asking for him, and that the rabbits were healthy and growing.

His mother also wrote, "There's no news on any front," by which Mike knew that she meant his father. "Tom De-

Witt stopped by, just to be friendly," she wrote. "He wanted to know how you were doing at school." She still didn't seem to know about DeWitt's idea that Glenn would try to contact Mike in Brookings, and her not knowing made it seem less possible. Mike had to remind himself that it could happen, that he needed to be on guard in case it did. Tom wouldn't have given him those phone numbers if he didn't think Glenn would show up. Or would he? Mike didn't trust DeWitt to be honest or straightforward about anything.

His mother ended her letter with, "I try not to look at your empty room when I walk past it." That had a strong effect on Mike. His room now seemed almost human. He imagined the room missing him as if it were a person. Mike had left his room behind, which made him feel as if he'd left himself behind.

Leaving McCrory Gardens, walking back across the hot campus, Mike threw his mother's letter into a Dumpster behind the Union. He kept Donetta's and, back in his room, tacked up her watercolor above his desk. He could hear Raymond next door, talking with their neighbors, Terry Linder and John Watts. The three of them had chemistry together. In a few minutes they'd probably come and ask Mike if he wanted to walk to Medary Commons for dinner. They were the only people Mike had met so far, except for a girl named Heather Coates, in his honors writing seminar, who also lived in Hansen Hall. She was tall and friendly and had spoken to him after class the day before.

The class was subtitled: "Writing about Crises of Faith and Ethics," and she had said, "I like Professor Jakes, but I've never had what you'd call a real crisis."

"Me either," Mike had lied, but a difference had established itself between them, separating him from her. His father's crime had given him less in common with almost everybody. And he never had felt that he was much like other people to start with.

Outside now the sun was low. Mike couldn't see it from his window, which faced south, but he could see the sky becoming paler, and the walls of his room changing from white to pale yellow.

He left before Raymond and the others could find him. He walked all the way to Larson Commons, near Sixteenth Avenue, where he was unlikely to know anyone. He got his tray of food and carried it to the far back corner. Three people at a nearby table looked up, then returned to their conversation. Most people were in groups or couples, but even the students sitting alone, like him, didn't seem particularly lonely. Mike felt the solitary way he usually did; it was just more noticeable to him now. It was like clouds parting so that you could see the moon, when you already knew the moon was there.

HE'D forgotten there was a party that night at his dorm. When he walked into the lobby, after supper, there were at least fifty people there, a table with punch and pizza rolls, and Dwight Yoakum playing on a boom box. Heather Coates was standing next to the front desk with her roommate, Morgan Gault—the pretty girl who had smiled at Mike at Mad Jack's. Heather waylaid Mike and introduced him to Morgan. Both girls were from Chamberlain.

"We've been best friends since the seventh grade," Morgan said. She had on a short skirt and a blouse that tied under her breasts, leaving her stomach bare. "I'm not an honors student, though," she told Mike. "Heather's the smart one."

"What one are you, then?" he asked.

She looked at Heather and they both laughed. "I'm the fun one," Morgan said. "I'm the one who goes on a date the night before I have a test."

John Watts came over to talk to Heather, and Morgan put her hand on Mike's arm. "Will you sneak outside with me so that I can smoke?"

"Why do we have to sneak?"

"We don't. I'm just used to it, from high school."

He left with her through the back door; she led him across the lit-up parking lot to the dark field on the other side. It was a clear night, with stars beginning to appear. She walked into the middle of the field before sitting down.

"Do you want one?" she asked, lighting a cigarette.

"No," he said. "Thanks."

"So you don't smoke."

"Not usually."

"What do you do usually?"

"Heroin."

"Not really."

"No," Mike said. "Not really."

It was deserted where they were—on the northern edge of campus, beyond which were only flat pastures owned by the university.

"I saw you at Mad Jack's Sunday night," Morgan said.

"I remember."

"I have a boyfriend at school in Sioux Falls," she told him. "But I'm not serious about him. I don't expect to marry him or anything like that." She put out her cigarette. She leaned back on her elbows, brushing her arm against Mike's. "I'm free to date other people."

"I don't like that word, *date*," Mike said. "It's a fruit, for one thing."

"How about 'fuck around with'?" Morgan said. "Do you like that better?"

It was something Donetta would have said, but only to him, and only after they had been dating for a long time. It was sexy, but weird, coming from somebody he hardly knew. He turned toward her and they kissed. She pressed herself against him. Her breasts were larger than Donetta's; she had wider shoulders and stronger arms, and as they kissed more deeply she reached down and put her hand on the crotch of his jeans.

"I want to jerk you off," she said, which startled him even more. She undid his jeans and slipped her hand into his underwear, and it was clear that she was practiced at doing it. After just a few minutes he was ready to come but didn't let himself. He reached up under her skirt and encountered thong-bikini panties—something he'd never seen on a girl except in magazines. He felt overstimulated and slightly crazy. When he couldn't help but come, she acted as if she did, too. Mike couldn't tell. Nothing about her seemed genuine.

He lay on the grass, breathing hard, looking up at the stars and moon. It was Lee-Ann who came into his mind, almost as if she were watching what he was doing. What would she say right now? he wondered. But he already knew. She'd say, "I don't think that's what you need." She'd say, "You have to separate people you can trust from people you can't."

Morgan smiled at him. "Next time we'll bring Kleenex," she said. She stood up and brushed off her clothes, then brushed off Mike's when he stood up.

"Get rid of the evidence, right?"

"There's nothing wrong with what we did," Morgan said coldly.

"I didn't mean that."

"All right," she said. "It's just that some guys are hypocritical about sex."

He walked her back to the party. They didn't talk, and once inside the lobby she moved away from him. He was both glad and hurt. He stood near Raymond, who was talking to a plain-looking girl named Carla Beeker. Mike recognized her from his writing seminar. She'd read aloud a journal entry about her brother, who had cystic fibrosis. She was, in fact, the only person in the class Mike could relate to, because she was thoughtful, and she didn't smile unless there was a reason to. You could tell by looking at her that she had serious things on her mind.

She and Raymond were talking about the valedictory speeches they'd given at their respective high schools. Conversations like that, Mike knew, were the kinds of things people made fun of straight-A students for. It made them seem like nerdy overachievers. But the people who made fun of them were idiots with inferiority complexes. Mike's problem was that he saw both groups critically. He could never be part of any group unself-consciously.

He went upstairs, turned on the light, and stood next to the phone. He hadn't written to Donetta yet, and he called her now.

"Hey," he said when she answered. "I thought you'd be on a date with some hotshot football player."

"Why would I be on a date with anyone?" she said.

"You wouldn't. I was just kidding."

"Why?" Donetta asked.

Mike didn't have an answer. He looked at his small room—the window too narrow to let in enough air, the beds suffocatingly close to the ceiling.

"Mike?" she said.

"Listen," he told her. "I just wanted to say thanks for the

letters. And for the drawing of the tree. I put it up over my desk." He stopped, listening to her breathe. "I don't know why I was joking like that," he said then. "I don't."

Raymond came in holding a box of pizza rolls. "They had them left over," he said, before seeing that Mike was on the phone.

"Your roommate?" Donetta asked.

"Yes."

"And there's no girl waiting for you?"

"Of course not."

"It's really hard," she told him, "being far from you. I knew it would be. But it's worse than I thought."

"For me, too," Mike said.

"Is it?"

"Sure."

After getting off the phone he stood at the window, looking at the flatness of the streets and the scattered lights of campus. Raymond, behind him, was sitting in front of a blank computer screen. "Is there a definite way to know if a girl likes you?" he asked Mike.

"I don't know about definite," Mike said. "You have to go with what it feels like. You have to trust your instincts."

Raymond laughed a little. "Then I'm really in trouble," he said.

They both settled down to study. Mike got out his honors writing anthology and read his assignment, "The Allegory of the Cave," by Plato, about how most people don't see the world but see only shadows of the world, and about how we should ascend into the light of intelligence and truth and see things as they really are.

What would that mean, Mike thought—that how things seemed were never how they really were? And that you couldn't believe that what you saw was what other people saw? And how could you stand to be objective anyway? For example, he knew what a creep he would look like to himself, right now, if he could see tonight objectively. Fortunately, he thought, there was no danger of that.

He gave up on reading and took refuge in daydreaming—imagining himself in the Badlands, high up, sitting still, waiting to see mountain goats. He'd never seen just one. They were always in pairs or groups of three. They had ways of communicating that were impossible for human beings to discover. They were mysterious to humans, and humans were mysterious to them. In that way Mike was safe from them. It was also a given that they were safe from him.

NINETEEN

MIKE'S life assumed a routine. He ate breakfast alone, unless he couldn't avoid Raymond; he attended his classes; and he had most of his other meals at the far end of campus. On the few occasions he went to dinner with Raymond and their neighbors, Terry and John, he listened more than he talked, especially when the subject was where each of them was from, or what their families were like. If they asked Mike a question, he answered in as few words as possible. On a Saturday night two weeks into the semester, he did talk a little about his job at the Schofields', as a way to describe his summer.

"That sounds great," Raymond said. "I spent all summer taking care of my stepbrother."

"I worked for my dad," John said. "It wasn't as bad as I thought it would be."

"I'd end up killing my dad if I had to work for him," Terry said. "Or he'd kill me."

They all laughed about that, Mike forcing himself to smile.

On that night he left the cafeteria earlier than they did and went to the library with his books. In terms of school he wasn't as on top of things as he might have been. "Learn your professors' names," Dr. Boyd had said. "Stay one class ahead with your reading and homework." Mike found the second part difficult to do.

Right now, in the library, he took a seat next to an open window, from where he could hear people playing soccer, in the dusk, in Sexauer Field. It was a warm night. The library was mostly empty. Mike opened his calculus book but became interested instead in the gray patterned carpeting and vacant carrels, then in the sound of the voices outside. He got up to get a drink of water and use the rest room. After that he made himself solve one problem before closing his book and returning to Hansen Hall.

On the fourth floor, in the hallway, Raymond, John, and two other honors students were trying to play hockey with umbrellas and a bar of soap. Raymond called a time-out, following Mike into their room. "Morgan Gault called," he told him. "She said for you to call her."

"Thanks."

"To call when you got back."

"Okay," Mike said. He put down his books, opened his

closet, and stuffed dirty clothes into a pillowcase. Laundry was something else that he hadn't stayed on top of.

Raymond was watching him. "She's really good-looking," he said.

"I guess so."

"But not very smart?"

"Smart enough."

"Her number's on the pad by the phone," Raymond told him.

Mike picked up his keys and opened the door.

"What should I tell her if she calls back?"

"Ask her out yourself," Mike said. He'd meant it to be funny, but it came out sarcastic and mean. "It doesn't matter," he told Raymond. "Say you haven't seen me."

DOWNSTAIRS, Mike had the laundry room to himself. He had brought along his calculus and world-history textbooks, which had been a mistake, he realized. Both books together made him feel overwhelmed. He should have brought one or the other. What he read instead were two *Sports Illustrated* magazines somebody had left behind.

When a Chinese student came in to collect her clothes from a dryer, Mike talked to her a little. She was small and slender, and her shiny hair reached almost to her waist. She said she was from Beijing. "What's it like to be so far from home?" he asked her.

"Not so bad. I get lots of letters from my family. And from my fiancé as well," she added shyly.

"Do you talk to them on the phone?"

"Almost never," she said. "It costs too much. You're lucky to attend school in your own country."

She finished folding her clothes and smiled at him. After she left he thought first about the letters from Donetta and his mother that he hadn't answered, and then about the Chinese girl. He got an erection imagining how, if she were undressed, her long hair would look against her skin. He considered masturbating, taking the risk of somebody walking in. It at least would differentiate how he spent a Saturday night from how he spent a weekday night. When two girls walked in a few minutes later, he wondered how he'd turned into such a pervert.

LATER, he went downstairs and outside, where streaks of clouds were blowing past a white moon. He wanted to get away from Raymond and the other people on the fourth floor. He walked down Seventh Avenue, past the rental houses close to the university, then past houses that were larger and nicer: older, two-story homes with cared-for lawns and big trees.

He could see into lighted living rooms and kitchens, and he imagined himself older, out of school, living alone in one of those houses. He'd put up a wooden fence people couldn't see through and get a dog; he wouldn't talk to anyone he didn't feel like talking to.

It was warm outside, not yet fall, not even at night. Donetta would like that, he thought. She hated the cold. For the previous Christmas, he'd bought her a down comforter with money he'd saved from the summer. She'd told him that on cold nights she'd get into bed early and look at the photo album her father had given her before he died—photographs he'd taken the year he was eighteen, hitchhiking cross-country by himself.

The pictures had titles like "Snowed-in in Greybull, Wyoming," or "Brush Mountain near Altoona, Pennsylvania." "It's like a diary," Donetta had said. She'd started one of her own, with a photograph of herself and Mike, at the lake, which she called, "In Love, at Crow Lake, South Dakota." Mike had had a copy of it once. He'd lost it, or thrown it out—he couldn't remember anymore. Early senility, he thought. Lose your mind at college.

When Mike got to Sixth Street he walked west, downtown, where the post office and restaurants were, small stores, and a bar called Ray's Corner, which had poker and blackjack machines. The streets were full of people. Mike didn't feel a part of the university or the town.

At the end of the wide street was Sexauer Feeds, a granary so big that Mike could see it all the way from his dorm window. That's where he could work, he thought, if he lived in one of those houses on Seventh Avenue. He could have a simple job, some repetitive thing he could do without thinking; then he could go home at night to his dog and his own peaceful house. He wouldn't have to lead a complicated life. His life could be as simple and quiet as that sheepherder's life in the book Josh had been reading. He could settle somewhere, draw a small circle around himself, as if with a compass, and live inside it.

Mike walked past the black, reflective glass of Mac's Retro-Rock-It Diner, where he hadn't eaten yet, though Raymond had asked him to several times. "They have good milk shakes," he'd told Mike. Mike pictured Raymond alone at a table, working on his space drawings, hardly looking up when the waitress came by.

Mike walked farther west, toward the railroad tracks and the airport. Away from the lights of Brookings, the moon was more distinct, but the clouds were increasing, and by the time Mike turned back toward the university there was no moon.

Most of the houses he'd walked past before were dark now; they weren't so inviting anymore. They could have been the houses in Mike's neighborhood in Wheatley— inhabited by people who were more screwed up than you wanted to know. Or else just boring.

A car drove by under the speed limit. Mike hardly noticed until it came around a second time. It was an Oldsmobile or a Buick, he thought, either brown or gray, and driven by a man, not a student. Mike kept walking, watching it inch toward the corner, then turn left and speed up slightly.

Don't be paranoid, he told himself. Someone was probably lost, or else maybe the driver thought Mike was somebody else. There were a lot of possibilities, except that none of them seemed likely. What seemed likely was that it was either the police or somebody connected to his father.

And the next moment Mike felt as lost and overcome with fear as he had that night standing next to Elk Creek. He stood rigidly, trying to remember that the sidewalk under him was solid, as was the earth, and that if he were dying, the earth would not be dying with him; it would stay whole and in place no matter what his heart did.

The fear faded by degrees, but this time more of it was left behind, and what went underground only went to some purgatorylike place. So that while he felt less afraid, he also knew that he wasn't the same anymore. He probably hadn't been for a while.

Hansen Hall was in front of him now, and he stood back from the lighted street, under an oak tree, waiting to see if the car came around a third time. He was across the street from the girls' side of the building; there were ten or twelve lighted windows with open curtains. He saw one girl in a nightgown, brushing her hair, another wearing only a sweatshirt and panties. If somebody was watching him, he thought, then they were watching him watch that.

He waited only a few seconds longer. Then he crossed the street, went inside and up the stairs.

.　　.　　.

EARLY Monday morning, by accident, and without wanting to, he ate breakfast with Heather Coates. He was sitting
alone at Medary Commons; she came through the cafeteria
line, saw him, then came over. "I don't know if I should sit
with you or not," she said. "You didn't call Morgan back."

"I meant to."

She took her juice and plate off her tray and sat down,
smoothing back her dark hair. "I guess I'll talk to you. But
not about that."

"About what then?" Mike said guardedly.

"I don't know. Anything. I don't have anything specific
in mind."

"Good."

"What do you mean?"

"Nothing," Mike said. "Just good." He watched her
butter her toast. His own plate of food was in front of him,
most of which he hadn't eaten.

"Aren't you hungry?" she said.

"Not really."

Heather ate all of her scrambled eggs before putting
down her fork. "Just tell me why you didn't call her back,"
she said.

"I thought you weren't going to talk about her."

"I know. I can't help it."

"Well, it was late," Mike said.

"What about all day yesterday, or last night?"

"So that makes me what?" Mike said. "An asshole?"

"I was thinking that you weren't one."

"So now I am."

"What do you think?"

"I might sound like one," Mike told her. "But that doesn't mean I am one. Like maybe I just have a lot on my mind."

"A lot of girls, you mean."

"Not quite," Mike said.

They sat in silence. Heather drank her juice.

"Did you read 'Fern Hill' yet?" she asked. It was a poem by Dylan Thomas, and was the next day's assignment for their writing class.

"I had to memorize it in tenth grade."

"You were lucky."

"Why?"

"Because it's like the best poem ever written."

"Who told you that?" Mike said.

"Nobody. I just like it."

"I'll read it again tonight."

"Before or after you call Morgan?" Heather said, and stood up to leave.

Fuck you, Mike said silently. He wasn't sorry for Morgan, but he was sorry he'd screwed around with her. It made him feel desperate for sex. Or just really, really depressed. He sat in the cafeteria a while longer, through his first class, in fact.

TWENTY

THE nights and mornings grew chilly. The leaves weren't changing yet, but in western South Dakota the temperature dropped into the thirties one night. Mike's mother called one morning just to say that. She called him often, reminding him to get the oil changed in his truck, to eat three meals a day, to get involved in extracurricular activities. He hadn't gone out for wrestling. Why would he have cared whether he won or lost a match?

"Aren't there clubs you can join?" his mother said one night on the phone. He'd fallen asleep at his desk; the telephone had woken him up. "Why not ask Dr. Boyd about it?" The head of the honors program, an agronomy professor, was boyish-looking and slight. All Mike knew about him was that he'd been on the rodeo circuit when he was young. Mike's mother seemed to believe that Boyd was the head/teacher/father/priest of the university—somebody Mike could go to for anything.

Mike's mother only mentioned his father once; she told Mike that the divorce would be final soon. Mike had not told her about the car following him. It had not happened again, as far as he knew, and he had been paying careful attention, both when he was walking and when he was driving. He'd told himself, finally, that there was no point in worrying. Mike didn't know anything. His father had never called him. Tom DeWitt had been wrong.

A sentence or two later, his mother told him that she'd been on a date. "I wasn't sure I should mention it," she said. "But I want you to know. I want to be honest with you. And I thought it might make you feel better, knowing that I had some company."

"Okay," Mike said. He didn't bother asking who it was. It was one more way Tom DeWitt was staying in their lives.

"All right, then," his mother said brightly. "So. How are your grades? What subject are you best in?"

"Physical education," Mike said.

His mother laughed. "I've missed your jokes," she told him.

Me, too, he thought.

When he got off the phone he became aware of voices next door—Terry's, John's, and Raymond's. They were talking seriously, it sounded like, and Mike thought he heard his name mentioned. He sat as still as he could, listening. But he didn't hear it again, and soon they began talking more casually.

THE following day, after Mike's classes were over and he was back at his dorm, checking his mail, a girl standing next to him said, "It's not here yet. It's late today." But there was an unstamped envelope in his mailbox. Morgan, he told himself, but it wasn't from Morgan, and his head started hurting the second he saw the name. He went out to the parking lot so that he could read the letter alone, in his truck. It was handwritten on plain white paper.

"We think that your father was on a bus in Illinois," Tom had written, "traveling north. He might be working his way up to you. If he is, and if he contacts you, you're going to have to make a decision. Think about it beforehand. He might not be that far away."

Enclosed, in case Mike had lost or thrown out the one he had, was a card with three phone numbers on it. At the bottom of the card Tom had written, "Don't forget what your father did," and, "Don't put yourself in the middle."

Two girls were getting into the car next to Mike's. The one who sat in the passenger seat smiled at him. He looked at her blankly, not recognizing her from one of his classes. He realized who she was as the car was backing out, and found himself raising his hand to wave at the empty space between his truck and a Pontiac.

·   ·   ·

HE read the letter several times, locked it in his glove compartment, and started driving slowly and nervously through campus and then through town, looking for Tom DeWitt's car.

It was a cool afternoon. Students were playing Frisbee under the elms near the bell tower, and a group of girls was jogging through campus. Mike drove through every university parking lot and in and out of the parking lots of every motel and restaurant in Brookings. He saw two state police cars near the stadium, on North Campus Drive—he never had seen any on campus before.

For all Mike knew, his father was already in Brookings, and Mike was being used as bait. Or else maybe DeWitt was testing him somehow, trying to figure out, in advance, what Mike would do. All Mike was sure of was that none of this was about him. Mike, as an individual, didn't matter to Tom DeWitt—not that Mike needed to, or expected to. But it was important for him to remember, because the thing that could fool you, Mike thought—or make a fool of you—was believing that people were thinking about you when they weren't, caring about you when they didn't.

He drove through campus a second time, and through Brookings again, ending up near the Best Western and the Wal-Mart as the streetlights were coming on. The line along the horizon was blue gray, the color of storm clouds over the Black Hills. But there were no hills in Brookings.

There was no place from where he could have seen far enough.

He drove back toward campus, the northern edge of which was barren-looking and unkempt. There was grass growing up through the tennis courts. There was the shiplike sports complex looking alien among the other buildings. There was no car he recognized, nobody following him or waiting for him at his dorm—just a note from Raymond, which said: "Went to dinner. Waited for you then gave up." He'd left the same note three times before.

LATER in the evening, while Raymond studied diligently and Mike lay in bed, doing nothing, Donetta called. "I'm failing precalculus," she said. "I don't ever want to hear the word *exponential* again. And what the hell is an imaginary number?

"Never mind," she said, when he started to answer. "I don't want to waste a phone call on it."

"Me either," Mike said. "Anyway, I can't remember what it means."

"Why not? What do you mean?"

Mike looked at Raymond, who looked back at Mike, picked up his book, and left the room. As soon as he was gone Mike turned off the light and stretched the telephone cord so that he could keep watch out the window for Tom DeWitt's car—for any suspicious-looking car. "I'm not doing too well in calculus," he told Donetta. "It's like I'm senile. Or stupid."

"Your mother says that you've been hard to talk to."

"Why are you talking to my mother about me?"

"I'm not," Donetta said. "But how can I help seeing her at school?"

"You could walk the other way." She was quiet, and Mike could hear Cory and Mrs. Rush arguing in the background.

"They've been doing that since breakfast," Donetta said. "I don't even know what about. I just stay in my room. I've been working part-time at Andell's to earn enough money to visit."

"No wonder you want to come here."

"No," she said. "I want to see you."

Mike was silent.

"I don't even know if you've kept your promise," Donetta said.

"About what?"

"About loving somebody else. And not making me figure it out."

"I don't love anybody else," Mike told her.

"What's wrong, then?"

"Who says anything is wrong?"

"You did," Donetta said. "About calculus."

"Well, that's just school," Mike said.

"It seems like more than that."

"Nothing that's wrong is about you," Mike told her. "Or

about you and me. Some things I have to handle on my own." Donetta was quietly listening. In the background he heard a door slam.

"Will you call me when you feel bad?" she asked him.

"I don't feel bad."

"But if you do," she said, "tell yourself what I do. That it's not a fact. It's just a feeling."

Mike watched a dark car go past the dorm and turn down Seventh Avenue.

"Mike?" Donetta said.

"Okay," he told her.

"But are you really listening to what I'm saying?"

"Yes. I heard you." Outside, the car kept going.

"It can really help," Donetta said. "Even though it might sound silly now."

"Listen," Mike told her. "I have to go. I have a lot of work to do. I'll talk to you soon, okay?"

Afterward, Mike made up his mind not to call her for a while, not to call anyone, or check his phone messages. Because it was too stressful to talk to people. They didn't understand how he felt. He was different now. The person they were talking to was not the person they had known in the summer. Maybe he hadn't been that person ever.

The door opened. It was Raymond, making sure that Mike was off the phone. "I understand about privacy," he told Mike. "Just tell me when you need it."

Mike nodded. He sat at his desk, which was piled up with books and assignments, all the work he didn't have the energy to do. He glanced out the window every few minutes. Then he searched through his desk for the five self-addressed envelopes Lee-Ann had given him. He thought that she might be the only person who could understand what he was going through.

"Dear Lee-Ann," he wrote. "I just wanted to say hello. I was wondering what was going on there and what Neil and Ed were up to. And you. Because I really haven't made any friends here."

He crossed out that last sentence. But there was nothing he could think of to replace it with.

TWENTY-ONE

O VER the next few weeks Mike got D's on two tests
and F's on three quizzes. He was too tired, for one thing,
and got winded climbing one flight of stairs, let alone the
four to his room. And he'd begun waking at four-thirty in
the morning and not falling back asleep. He'd hear the first
birds sing and lie with his eyes closed as the darkness
turned to light. His dreams stayed vividly in his mind. A
few days earlier, after receiving a letter from the Schofields—with Janna's scribbling at the bottom of the page
—he dreamed that the rabbits born under their porch had
been born dead. In a more recent dream he was a child, and
his father was teaching him how to swim in the deep end
of a pool. "See how long you can hold your breath," his father told him. *

He'd stopped answering the phone or checking his messages, though he still read his letters. Donetta wrote him almost every day, and his mother wrote often as well. In his mother's most recent letter she asked him to make sure his answering machine was working. She also told him that she'd been on two more dates, and he read that part of her letter closely.

"I had a good time," she wrote. "What I mean is that it's somebody I'd like to keep on seeing. And I'd like you to meet him, Mike. It doesn't have to be anytime soon. I don't mean that. But Jim has heard a lot about you."

It was the student she was tutoring, and not Tom De-Witt. Instead of relief Mike felt that he'd fallen backward again, that he was falling behind at the same speed that his life, and the lives of the people around him, were moving forward.

ON the third Thursday of October, a mild morning, the sun shining down on the autumn trees, Mike was late—again—for his Honors Writing Seminar. He took a seat in the back of the room; Professor Jakes looked up but said nothing. They were discussing *Spiritual Autobiography,* by Simone Weil. Mike had read it twice, trying to understand it, and unlike his other homework, it remained in his head.

"Why did she think so much about God?" one person asked.

"Because she thought so much about dying," Heather Coates said.

" 'If only I knew how to disappear,' " Professor Jakes read, " 'there would be a perfect union of love between God and the earth I tread, the sea I hear. . . . I disturb the silence of heaven and earth by my breathing and the beating of my heart.' That's from a journal she kept," he told the class. "What do you think she's saying?"

"That she hated herself," somebody said. "That she thought the world would be a better place if she died."

"Except that she believed in love," said Carla Beeker.

"If she lived now," a boy asked, "wouldn't we think she was crazy?"

"Don't you ever think about who you are?" Carla said. "Or about God? Or about the kind of life you should lead?"

"No more than I have to."

People laughed. Mike looked at the phrases he'd underlined in his book: *I always believed that the instant of death is the center and object of life. If I am sad, it comes primarily from the permanent sadness that destiny has imprinted on my emotions . . . ; Ideas come and settle in my mind by mistake, then realizing their mistake, they absolutely insist on coming out. . . .*

"What do you think, Mr. Newlin?" Professor Jakes asked.

Mike looked up. "I don't know," he said slowly. "There's something personal about the way she says things. You feel like you know her when you read this."

"Because she feels things so strongly," Carla said. "Like how she read that one poem over and over."

"Did anyone look up the poem?" Professor Jakes asked.

Carla held up a thick volume of poetry, and everyone laughed, including her. Professor Jakes asked her to read it.

In a soft voice she read: " 'Love bade me welcome: yet my soul drew back, Guiltie of dust and sinne. . . .' " And Mike's eyes filled with tears, though he wasn't sure what, exactly, the poem was about. He sat low in his chair, holding his book up in front of him, trying to focus on something else. But everything hurt to think about: his father, his mother at home, Donetta alone at night in her room, writing letters to Mike that he didn't answer.

Behind his thoughts Carla was gently saying, " 'Love took my hand, and smiling did reply,/Who made the eyes but I?' " And Mike, closing his own eyes, thought of the moon rising over the Black Hills into the wide dark sky. " 'And know you not, sayes Love, who bore the blame?' " And Mike was thinking of the long shadows on the backyard grass, and antelope coming into the fields at dusk, and himself, always watching, always distant, always far away.

" 'You must sit down, sayes Love, and taste my meat:/So I did sit and eat.' " That was the last line of the poem. The class was over. Mike left first, hurrying out into the hall, down the stairs, and into the sunlight.

HE didn't attend his other classes. Instead, he went back to Hansen Hall, put his books in his truck, and unloaded his motorcycle from the back of it. He hadn't ridden it since he'd come to Brookings. He'd been too distracted, or even somehow too afraid. But now the only thing on his mind was getting away from Brookings and from his life there.

He rode east on Highway 14, stopping first to buy gas. Inside, as he paid, the girl behind the counter said, "Are you a student?" She had on a South Dakota State sweatshirt. He nodded. "Me, too," she said. "I study between customers." She was freckled and overweight, with long, braided hair. "It's a different world in here," she told him. "It's like what I read about." She held up a psychology textbook.

"I bet," Mike said. Outside, two hunters in a mud-splattered pickup were pulling up to the air hose.

"I hate hunters the most," the girl said. "I hate when they drive in with deer strapped to their cars."

"Well, I don't hunt," Mike said.

"That's what I thought. I try to figure out things about the people who come in here. Only usually I never know if I'm right." Mike stood there, waiting for his change. "Do you want to know what I think about you?"

He didn't. But he said, "I guess."

"That you're skipping class. And you're not very happy."

"I'm just worried about something," he said.

She gave him his change, and as he turned to leave she handed him two candy bars. "In case you're worried because you're hungry," she told him.

Outside he straddled his motorcycle, watching the highway and watching the hunters. He'd lied inside. He'd gone hunting with Josh and Josh's father a few times, and twice with Neil and Ed Schofield. He'd shot a pheasant. His father had hunted from the age of ten, or so he'd said, but he'd never suggested doing it with Mike. He was scornful of people who did it in groups. "You have to hunt alone," he used to say. "It's a solitary activity."

That's what Mike was thinking about when he saw, or thought he saw, Tom DeWitt's car, traveling west. It wasn't a distinctive car, and it wasn't close enough for him to be sure. Mike's hands were shaking, though, and he pulled onto the highway in the direction he'd just come from and rode, fast, through Brookings and all the way past Highway 81 without seeing Tom's car or one like it again. It must not have been DeWitt, Mike thought, but he rode through town and through campus before deciding to just say fuck it. What would he do anyway, if he did see him?

He headed east again, riding past the gas station and into the country. The road was bright with sun, and on either side were cow pastures and hay fields. He hadn't brought his helmet and felt nothing but sun and wind, heard nothing but the noise of the engine. Instead of campus buildings and students he saw farmhouses and grazing cows and horses. The road unfolded in front of him as endlessly as the way he used to imagine the future.

He turned onto a smaller highway marked SCENIC and accelerated, following the center line closely and leaning far in on the curves. In his head was a sentence from the essay they'd discussed in his writing seminar, the first sentence he'd underlined: "I always believed that the instant

of death was the center and object of life." Mike kept saying that to himself, even though he'd never believed in
heaven, not even as a kid. He wished there was something
he felt that sure of, that he'd always known, always understood.

He accelerated again and felt the candy bars fall out of
his pocket. He hadn't wanted them anyway, and it was
none of that girl's business whether he was happy or not,
hungry or not. She'd wanted him to respond to her in some
way, and he was tired of people wanting reactions from
him. The more detached you were, the more people wanted
to get attached to you. You were the center and object for
them, but you didn't have a center for yourself; you were
too busy being theirs.

A pickup rushed toward him, then past him, and then a
white car. Tom DeWitt will probably come along next,
Mike thought, or else Mike's father, in a car belonging to
some new woman gullible or dumb enough to help him,
and as Mike downshifted on the next curve his rear wheel
locked and he didn't pull the clutch in fast enough.

He lost control, the bike just going out from under him.
It seemed prolonged, and there was a second when it felt
more like being super alive than having an accident. He
stayed with the bike as long as he could—too long—then
jumped clear of it as it slid down into a dry ditch. He
landed facedown in the grass.

The world was suddenly still and suddenly silent.
Would death feel like this? Mike wondered. But the com-

plications of his mind and heart were already flooding in, and so was the pain he felt—in his right shoulder, and leg, and particularly in his grass-burned hands, which he must have put down first, trying to break his fall. He sat up and took stock of himself. His jeans and jacket were torn, but none of his bones seemed broken. It took him a minute to stand up. Then shakily and gingerly he slid down into the ditch to check his bike, which was less damaged than he was, and rideable.

He slowly climbed up the other side of the embankment. The barbed-wire fence was stretched enough, in one spot, for him to get through, and he carefully lay down in the field grass, looking up at hawks gliding in the blue sky. It took a long time for his heart to stop racing. He told himself that he wouldn't have to move until he felt like it. He could stay there all day, if he wanted to, and even into the night. He could stay there forever. After a while he fell asleep, dreaming that a car he was in, driven by his father, was speeding out of control. Mike jerked awake. Just watch the hawks, he told himself—the way they rise and fall with the air currents, the way they dip and climb.

HE rode back to Brookings. He'd come farther than he'd realized, and now he hardly noticed the straw-colored fields or the farmhouses. He had the glare of the sun in his eyes until the sun dropped below the horizon; then the air turned substantially colder.

At Hansen Hall he left his bike next to his truck, and up in his room he got into bed without undressing. He pretended to be asleep when Raymond came in an hour later, followed by Terry Linder, who said, "Want some dinner?"

They left, and Mike heard Raymond say, in the hallway, "It's like I don't have a roommate."

Then Mike was left alone with his imagination: himself on his bike on that scenic road—except that this time, when he lost control, he skidded into the other lane where there was a truck, and when he collided with the truck his body was mangled like in a horror movie. The truck driver called the police, who called Mike's mother, and though she was sad for a while she at least didn't have to worry about him anymore; and when his father found out—assuming he ever went to that trouble—he felt bad that he'd given Mike leukemia, a deadly disease even if Mike was recovering from it, and maybe his father tried to kill himself, probably without success.

The main thing was that Mike finally would be able to fuck up, fuck himself up, and in that instant be through with everything. Any other way you fucked up, you had to pay the consequences afterward. Fucking up just partway meant that you were still trying to hold things together. It was even worse, because the more you fucked up, the more pieces there were to hold together. So the only real freedom was to completely let it go—fuck your family, fuck your life, fuck yourself.

Ideas come and settle in my mind by mistake. . . . He was like that writer. He thought he understood what she was saying.

_____

TWENTY-TWO

IN the morning Mike stayed in bed until he was sure he would have the bathroom to himself. He hurt more today. He was better after his shower, though so tired that he sat in his desk chair for twenty minutes before getting dressed. He ate cold cereal in his room, then went to the classes he hadn't missed already.

In his biology class he sat in a back corner and tried writing a letter to Donetta, getting as far as, "I know I haven't written much" and "I don't have much to say," before giving up and looking out the window. There was a strong wind blowing, and torn-looking clouds were moving fast from the west. The temperature was twenty degrees colder than it had been the day before.

While the professor at the lectern talked about Darwin, Mike drew pictures in the margins of his notebook—nothing you could recognize, he knew, nothing as good as Donetta's drawings, which always had a feeling to them; you could tell what she felt by what she drew. The high school art teacher had told her, "Be disciplined. Use your brain." Mike thought that he was wrong. Donetta had her own way of being intelligent. He looked down at his letter, thinking that if he never saw her again, how would she know that he'd finally understood that?

He reread his sentences and crossed out the three *I*'s. They said and meant nothing, and drew too much attention to themselves. They were like black lines of paint on a white wall. As long as he had to use that word, he thought, there was no point in writing letters to anyone.

IT was four o'clock when he returned to his room and discovered a note on his desk from Raymond: "Dr. Boyd called. He wants you to come by Solberg Hall. He said it was important."

As Mike hurried across campus, he told himself what must have happened: Either his father had shown up in Brookings and been arrested, or worse; or Tom DeWitt was setting a trap for Mike's father right now, one that he was involving Mike and Dr. Boyd in as well. Mike should have stayed home in Wheatley, as he'd wanted to, no matter what his mother had said. His father's belongings were already out of her way, in the basement. She'd never have to see Glenn again unless she wanted to. For Mike it was different.

Dr. Boyd's door was open, but he was with a student. He looked up and said, "Give me five minutes."

Too jittery to wait in the hall, Mike walked outside and stood on the top step, shifting from one foot to the other. The wind in the elms was shaking loose the leaves, and dark clouds sailed past overhead. Students were walking along the sidewalks and cutting across the grass. The gap between himself and them had grown too wide for Mike to cross.

"Mike?" Dr. Boyd was holding open the door for him.

"What's wrong?" Mike said.

"Come on in first." He led Mike down the hall and into his office. The building was old and the room was large, with a casement window that overlooked the street. He closed the door and asked Mike to sit down. "It's not an emergency," he told him then. "I just thought we could talk."

Mike took a deep breath, tried to calm down. "About what?" he said.

"I thought we could talk about a few things," Dr. Boyd said again. He sat at his desk, looking down at an open folder. "Grades, for one thing."

"They'll get better," Mike said. "I got off to a slow start."

"It's not just that. You've missed classes. You've been late to the ones you do attend. I'm concerned about how you're doing in general."

"I'm all right," Mike said.

Dr. Boyd closed the folder and rested his arms on it. "Your mother phoned me before the semester started," he told Mike. "But I already knew. I'd read about it in the paper."

"When?" Mike said.

"When it happened. Not lately. I haven't seen anything about it since then."

Mike was too upset to speak. He looked out the window at traffic passing by in the street. "I don't want people to know," he said finally. "It's private."

"I can understand that," Dr. Boyd said. "But maybe you and I could talk about it. About the effect it's having on your schoolwork."

"It's not having an effect," Mike said.

"Have you discussed your grades with your professors?"

Mike shook his head, feeling tears rising. He put his hand over his mouth, pretending to cough, and remembered too late about the bruises.

"How did you hurt yourself?" Dr. Boyd asked.

"A bike accident," Mike said. "No big deal." He looked away again, this time at a filing cabinet, on which there was a framed photograph: a woman and two boys on the front porch of a two-story house.

"My family," Dr. Boyd said kindly.

"Your house reminds me of ours," Mike said, humiliated to hear his voice catch on the "ours."

"We've lived in it since our sons were born," Dr. Boyd

said. "Fourteen years." He smiled at Mike. "Time goes by faster as you get older. It helps you put things in perspective."

From the hallway came the sound of doors closing, and footsteps. "Friday," somebody said. "Time to party." The cheerfulness of the voice sounded alien to Mike, almost inconceivable. The room was growing dim, the light outside less bright. Dr. Boyd reached toward his desk lamp, then seemed to reconsider.

"You should talk with your professors, Mike," he said. "Or I could, with your permission."

"No. Thanks."

"You can come over here anytime, just to talk."

"Okay."

"Or I could refer you to someone—a psychologist, for example. I don't mean right now. But if you ever think it might be useful."

Mike shook his head, keeping it down, keeping Dr. Boyd from seeing his eyes. "Is that it, then?" he asked.

"I'd like to help."

"I don't need help."

"Maybe there's something else I could do that I haven't thought of."

"No," Mike told him. "I'm okay."

Dr. Boyd looked at him, not speaking. Mike concentrated on the window, then the office floor, which was clean and wavy with wax—like the kitchen floor at home. Then Dr. Boyd rose, walked to the door, and opened it. He said good-bye to Mike, and Mike felt himself being watched as he walked down the hallway toward the double glass doors and went outside.

The sun was down, and the wind was blowing carpets of leaves into the street. Mike's shoulder and leg were sore; he hadn't worn his jacket, and he was cold. He walked past couples holding hands, past small groups of talkative girls. Unexpectedly, pieces of "Fern Hill" came into his mind: "rivers of the windfall light," and "nightly under the simple stars." He didn't know what came before, in between, or after, but the poem was about time, he knew—how it kept you captive, because you were always dying, even from the beginning, even before you realized it.

IN Mike's dorm room, Raymond was sitting on the rug beneath the beds, with three books open in front of him, working on a paper. "Do you want to get dinner?" he asked Mike.

"I don't think so. I'm not hungry." Mike walked around him.

Raymond said, "You know, you should eat sometimes. You should call people back, too. You've got five messages."

"I'll listen to them later."

Raymond pushed back his limp hair. "Look," he said. "People are worried about you."

"Like who?" Mike said.

"I don't know. Your mom. Your girlfriend, if that's who she is." He gestured to the phone machine with his pen, which flew out of his hand. He didn't move to retrieve it.

"I have things on my mind," Mike said.

"What things?"

"Just some private things."

"Well, I can't make you tell me," Raymond said. "But I know what it's like to feel bad. I didn't talk about it either. I just waited for it to get better."

Mike nodded.

"It takes a long time that way," Raymond said.

Mike retrieved Raymond's pen. "Okay," he said. "I know."

"So let's go eat," Raymond said insistently. "We'll just go to Medary Commons." He stood up and got his jacket. He opened the door without giving Mike a chance to say no.

The night had grown wintry. They walked down Eleventh Street with their hands in their pockets, into the wind, which blew in gusts. "It's supposed to snow tonight or tomorrow," Raymond told Mike. "Can you believe that? It's a good thing we don't have to go anywhere."

At Medary Commons they got their food and chose a table against the far wall. Mike, not hungry to start with, was too tired to eat. He tried hard to act normal. "How are your classes?" he asked Raymond.

"Pretty good except chemistry. At this point I'm hoping for a B."

"Everybody says that honors chemistry is a bitch."

"How are yours?"

"I've screwed up some tests," Mike said, with difficulty. "I think I can make up for them later."

Raymond focused on people coming through the cafeteria line, then said, "I asked Carla Beeker out. We went to eat one night."

"How was it?"

"Tense," Raymond said. "I mean for me. But she's easy to talk to," he told Mike. "She thinks I'm smart. And she knows what sad is."

Tears came to Mike's eyes immediately. He put down his fork, drank his water, and told himself: It's only a feeling. It's not a fact. That helped, but barely.

After Raymond finished eating he looked at Mike's plate—chicken, mashed potatoes, and green beans, mostly untouched. "Clean-plate club," he said. "You're not a member."

"What?"

"How my mother used to get me to eat."

They returned their trays, crossed the emptying room, and walked back to Hansen Hall through the windy night.

LATER, while Raymond worked on his paper, Mike read history—the fall of the Roman Empire. Out the window two girls were walking down Eleventh Street toward the dorm; as they passed under a streetlight, he saw that they were Heather Coates and Morgan Gault. The person Mike used to be would have had more sex, by now, with at least one of them. Not that he liked either of them much. But that wasn't as important as people thought. What was important was that you kept doing things in the world, making things happen. That's what history was about. You couldn't stop just because you didn't feel like waking up or talking to people, or because nothing seemed to matter to you anymore.

Mike shut his book and turned off his desk lamp.

"You're done?" Raymond said.

"Not exactly. I'm resting." He got into bed.

"I can turn off the light, go to the library."

"No," Mike said. "Study for both of us." He lay in his clothes on top of the covers. There seemed to be nothing ahead for him except cold weather, poor grades, and conversations that left him upset. He listened to Raymond leafing through the pages of his books. Raymond seemed pathetic to Mike, despite the fact that he did well in school and had friends and now might have a girlfriend. Raymond couldn't see the sorrowfulness of his life the way that Mike could. Raymond couldn't see the pointlessness of college.

Mike tried to concentrate on things that once had made him feel good. But swimming naked with Donetta or drinking whiskey with Josh belonged to some past life that didn't seem to be his anymore. He didn't fantasize about Lee-Ann anymore, and she probably didn't about him, and when Mike thought about sex it didn't drive away his other thoughts, the way it used to. If Raymond weren't there, he could masturbate. But maybe he wouldn't. Maybe he wouldn't even bother.

He got out of bed to get another blanket just as the phone rang.

"Mike?" his father said. "Drive on out! Did you forget about us, man? Come on! We're waiting for you!"

TWENTY-THREE

Outside, nothing was different—just the lit-up parking lot and the dark field behind it. Raymond had said, "Who was that?" and Mike had said, "My friend Josh. He's at the campgrounds with some friends. I'm driving out there."

Mike stood now at the back door of Hansen Hall, thinking: Maybe that hadn't been his father on the phone. Maybe Mike's own paranoia had changed one person's voice into another. But he wasn't that crazy.

He tried to think coherently. He had Tom DeWitt's card in his wallet, but there was no way he was going to call him. He didn't have any specific information, anyway. He didn't know where his father was or even where he, himself, was supposed to go. Still, he didn't want to be in this alone. He needed somebody to know. If he called Donetta, she'd freak out and call his mother. Josh would keep it to himself, but it was a weekend night and it was unlikely that he'd be home. Mike went to the pay phone in the lobby and called him anyway. There was no answer, not even an answering machine. He called again with the same result.

Behind him, three girls were laughing at something on television. The student working the desk had his head down, studying. Mike stood again at the back door, concentrating on the night outside. He waited. Then he walked out, unlocked his truck, and got in. If his father drove up now, he thought, they could talk right there, in the parking lot. Mike could find out exactly what had happened with Mary Hise, and what it was, if anything, his father wanted from him now. He could learn what the truth was without having to get too involved.

He sat for a long time, looking out, starting the engine when he got too cold. The wind was blowing hard enough, at moments, to rock the truck. Nobody drove up or walked past.

Then, across the wide field that separated Hansen Hall from its neighbor, Berg Hall, a car flashed its lights twice. Mike tensed up and watched. He hardly breathed. A minute passed, and the lights flashed twice again.

Okay, Mike thought. He would drive over there. His father, if it was his father, was afraid, probably, to come to Hansen Hall itself. They could talk there, then, in that parking lot. And if that car had no connection to his father, which was what Mike hoped, Mike would come back, go up to his room, and wait for his father to call again. Then if his father wanted to talk to him, he'd have to do it on Mike's terms, either on the phone or in the lobby, or in the parking lot of Hansen Hall. If talking to Mike was important enough, his father would have to take one of those options.

But as Mike drove toward Berg Hall, the car, flashing its lights only once this time, pulled out in front of him on Eleventh Street and kept going. When Mike got closer he saw that the only visible occupant was the driver, who was small and female. The car was a two-door, hatchback Toyota. It had an Illinois license plate, and Mike memorized it. He repeated it out loud while following the car through town, up one street and down another—a circuitous route, Mike thought, like in a detective movie. He was the private detective on the trail of the criminal's girlfriend. It felt a lot less fictional when he followed the car into the parking lot of a Taco Bell and saw his father run out of the restaurant. It stopped seeming like a game then. His father had a beard now, looked thinner, and was wearing a dark nylon jacket. He was holding a take-out sack and didn't look in Mike's direction. He opened the passenger door of the Toyota, and the driver accelerated the second he closed it.

Then they were on the entrance ramp to the interstate, heading south, and Mike, behind them, knew that he'd gone too far. He'd get off at the next exit, he told himself, but the car his father was in was not getting off; it was going exactly sixty-seven miles per hour, and if Mike didn't follow it, the space between himself and his father would widen to infinity.

He drove past the exit. In his rearview mirror he saw the lights of Brookings grow distant; in front of him he saw what he didn't know grow closer.

Halfway to Sioux Falls the Toyota left the interstate, heading east on a two-lane road and crossing the state line into Minnesota. That made it much worse, Mike knew, whatever crime this was that he was committing. But he couldn't stop. It was one thing to be afraid, he thought, but another thing to be a coward, and in addition it was his father he was following, not some maniac or stranger, and his father was the only person who could tell Mike what really had happened with Mary Hise. Mike was the only one who could find out. He could accomplish what no one else could.

He followed them through forty miles of countryside and one-stoplight towns, turning, finally, onto a long dirt road that ended at a semicircle of concrete-block cabins called the Twilight Lake Motel. There seemed to be no one staying there except them.

Mike's father jumped out of the car and ran back to Mike's truck. "Turn off your headlights and pull around behind the motel," he said. "As far back under the trees as you can. I'll meet you there."

He pointed to a rutted, overgrown trail that led through pine trees and ended an eighth of a mile into the woods. Without headlights Mike had to inch down it, and when he got out of his truck he knew the lake was close by: He heard water rippling and smelled the wetness. The night was absolutely black and cold. Then his father appeared, carrying a flashlight, a wrench, and a Minnesota license plate. "Here we are," he said, and grasped Mike's shoulders in an awkward hug. Mike didn't step away, but he kept his own arms at his sides. Then his father eyed the truck. "This is nice," he said. "Looks dependable. And it doesn't stand out." Then he stooped down behind the truck and loosened the bolts.

"Wait," Mike said. "I'm not staying. I'm going back to school tonight."

His father didn't move or lift his head. "No," he said. "I've got enough on my hands as it is."

"I'm just saying that I can't stay."

His father stood up. "Are you wearing a watch?" Pointlessly, because it was too dark for Mike to read it, he showed Mike his. "We won't have time to talk tonight," he said. "I won't be able to tell you what happened. We'll talk in the morning, then you'll go back first thing."

"Then I don't need a different license plate."

"Here's where I know more than you do," he told Mike. "A minute's work can save you heartache." He handed Mike the flashlight. "Hold it still," he said. "Keep it steady." He replaced Mike's South Dakota plate with the Minnesota one. "Welcome to the North Star State," he said. "Here. Put yours under the seat. We'll replace it when you leave."

"In the morning," Mike said.

"Fine. Whatever." Glenn stood up and took the flashlight from Mike. He turned it off and walked toward the motel. Mike hung back under the trees. "Mike!" his father said. Then he was walking again, with Mike behind him, trying to find his way in the darkness.

Ahead of them then was a bright rectangle of an open door and the sound of a radio, and then Mike was inside, facing a woman who looked as old as his father but was the size of a ten-year-old. She was so skinny that the outline of her shoulder blades was visible through her flowered top. "This is Inez," his father said, shutting and locking the door behind him.

She touched Mike's arm. "I guess you're real!" she said, then sat down in a dilapidated armchair. Then she was up again, moving into the adjoining kitchenette. She took a cigarette from her purse and lit it at the gas stove. "You two go on and talk," she said. "Just pretend I'm not here." She slid herself up on the counter and let her high-heeled sandals drop. Her toenails were painted pink. Her feet were so pale that Mike could see the blue of her veins.

The cabin was shabby, small, and old. There was only one bed, and Glenn, sitting down on the side that was farthest from the kitchenette, motioned for Mike to sit next to him. The heater came on noisily.

"Tell me what's going on at home," he said softly. "Keep your voice down. Inez doesn't know the details."

"Mom's okay," Mike said.

"Fine. Good. But I mean, as far as I'm concerned." He was leaning forward, his eyes intense and excited. His face was thin. He looked older, and his beard was more gray than brown. His left eye was bloodshot.

"Well," Mike said, "people know what you did."

"I didn't have to see you to find that out." He put his hand on Mike's knee. "It wasn't what they think, though. They're after me for the wrong thing."

The heater turned off. Glenn swiftly reached for the transistor radio and turned it up.

"You mean you didn't kill her?" Mike whispered.

His father jerked back around. "Listen," he said quietly. "She died, and I was there. But *kill* is the wrong word."

Behind them Inez jumped off the counter and opened the refrigerator. "How about eggs?" she said with her back to them.

"What?" Glenn said.

"Eggs," Inez said loudly.

"Where are the tacos?" Glenn said. "What happened to the Mexican food?"

"How should I know?"

"What's the right word, then?" Mike said in a low voice. "What word would you use?"

"I'd just as soon not use a word," his father said. "A word can mean one thing when you mean another."

"Did you shoot her or not?" Mike whispered.

"It's not that simple. You're asking the wrong questions. I can see already that you have bad information." Mike watched him rub the back of his neck, then move his head back and forth. "I get stiff," he told Mike. "It's tension. You'll find out about it when you get older."

"I find out about it every day," Mike said.

His father stared at him.

"I can do scrambled," Inez called out. "I can do over easy."

"What?" his father said.

"Scrambled, then," she said. "People who don't answer don't get what they want." After a moment she sang, along with the radio, "It hurts as much in Texas as it did in Tennessee."

"Tell her how good the meal is," Mike's father said. "Don't forget. Say it a couple of times."

TWENTY-FOUR

THEY ate at the Formica table in the kitchenette: eggs, toast, and milk on the verge of going sour. "Drink it anyway," Glenn told Mike. "It won't kill you."

"It's yogurt," Inez said happily. She crossed her thin legs, and Mike saw her slide a bare foot along Glenn's calf. "I have the coldest feet. So did my dad. We had that in common."

"Put on socks," Glenn said.

"Your dad's not a good listener," Inez told Mike. "But I guess you already know that. You have a whole history, you and your dad." With her toast she moved her eggs from one side of the plate to the other.

"This is good, isn't it, Mike?" Glenn said. He was eating with intensity. "It's delicious, isn't it?"

"Yes," Mike said. "Thank you."

"Then finish it," Inez said.

"I'm not all that hungry," Mike told her.

"Eat it anyway," his father said tersely.

Inez inched her own plate toward the center of the table. "I like history more than your dad does," she told Mike. "I'm interested in facts, like where somebody comes from, and who his people are."

"We have all day tomorrow to talk," Glenn said. "Let's just relax right now. Mike's tired."

"Why aren't those words coming out of Mike's mouth?" Inez said.

"Because it's full of your good food!" Glenn said with fake cheeriness.

Inez studied his face, then Mike's. "All right then," she said. Her eyes moved back and forth between them as they ate. Then she cleared the dishes while Glenn unrolled a sleeping bag at the foot of the bed. "It's where our dog would sleep if we had one!" Inez joked to Mike, who hadn't moved, who felt stunned and exhausted.

"You don't even like dogs!" Glenn said, steering her away from the kitchenette sink. It was apparent to Mike that he was moving fast to get her out of the kitchenette, then in and out of the bathroom. He did the same thing with Mike.

"How about this?" his father said to him, pointing with the toe of his shoe to the sleeping bag, which Mike got into—automatically and obediently, he realized, as if he were a dog—without undressing. Within a few minutes the light was off and the room was quiet. His father and

Inez, in the double bed, above him, seemed to fall asleep within minutes.

The situation was really wrong, really off kilter. It was so much crazier than Mike had expected that he couldn't keep up with it, especially because he was so tired. What had he expected? he thought then. Nothing. He hadn't had time to expect anything. But all he had to do was sleep, he thought. He would be out of there in the morning.

Except that he was almost too tired to sleep. The floor was cold; the sleeping bag was a cheap one, just thin polyester, and if Mike could have been anywhere right then, it would have been with Donetta under the comforter he'd given her—though not at her house, he thought—someplace else, someplace alone. Mike was the only person who had ever made Donetta feel less alone. Why did that mean so much to him? It came back to him often, how she'd said that on their first date, how she'd trusted him that much, as opposed to now, when she didn't anymore, when she'd gotten smart enough, he thought, not to.

He was lying on his back, tears making a path out of the corners of his eyes and wetting his hair. There were tears in everything, he thought, if you looked around you, if you saw the truth behind your situation and the sadness that was always behind the truth. Because underneath, you were tied to the world and to yourself, and who you were had already been decided beforehand, and without you.

In his sleep, Mike's father said, "Forget it," then, awake, he got out of bed. Mike heard the floor creak under his weight, then heard water running in the kitchenette sink. His father had always gotten up at night—to use the bathroom, to get a drink, to wander through the house in a lost way. He'd done it all Mike's life. Sometimes Mike had woken at two or three in the morning to the sound of his parents talking—his mother's voice more frequent, somewhat comforting, his father's hollow and depressed.

His father came to the foot of the sleeping bag. "Mike," he whispered; Mike kept his eyes closed. His father knelt down and shook him. "Mike," he whispered more loudly, and Mike was forced to open his eyes, to get up and follow his father into the kitchenette. "Keep an eye on Inez," his father said. "Though she sleeps soundly. She takes something."

"Where did she come from?"

His father hesitated. "I don't want to be cruel. I'll just say, she's helping me and I'm helping her." He put his hand on Mike's arm. "Did you tell anyone you were leaving?"

"My roommate."

"Who did you say I was?"

"Josh."

"When did you say you'd be back?"

"Last night," Mike lied.

"Call tomorrow and say Sunday."

"I can't."

"I'm asking you to, if it's not a risk to me."

"I don't want to," Mike said.

"Are you afraid of the police? Do you think that anyone

would fault a son for wanting to see his father?" He tightened his hand on Mike's arm. "I go from place to place," he said. "I hide by moving. You don't know how hard it is." He broke into tears.

Mike looked away from him, at the cold, dark room.

"Just stay until Sunday," his father said.

"Glenn?" Inez said. She got out of bed. She stood, shivering, in a long, white sweatshirt, her thin legs bare.

"It's okay, honey. Everything's fine. No problem of any kind." Glenn squeezed Mike's arm. "Sleep on it," he whispered, and followed Inez back to bed.

"Warm up my icy feet," Mike heard her say.

Mike lay back down. The wind outside had increased. There was no light yet, but he knew that it wasn't far away. The room was growing shadowy. It was the time of morning he'd been waking up at school, in his small, bare dorm room. But that room didn't seem so bare to him now, nor did his life at school: walking to his classes, returning to Hansen Hall afterward, and opening his mailbox, hoping to find what he almost always did—an envelope addressed to him in Donetta's small, back-slanted handwriting. Even the nights there seemed less lonely now.

It didn't matter anymore how unhappy he'd been in Brookings. That had been his life, and now he felt on the verge of losing it. He was missing it as if it had been lost.

TWENTY-FIVE

MIKE woke alone, after ten. The day outside was overcast and blustery, and there was a note for him on the unmade bed: "Don't leave. Dad." Inez's car was gone. The first thing Mike did was check his jacket to make sure that his father had not taken his truck keys.

In the kitchenette he ate two doughnuts from a package on the counter and was in the bathroom, throwing up, a minute later. Then, not feeling much better, he got into the shower, standing under the hot water until it ran cold. He dressed and walked out to his truck. He was unlocking the door to get aspirin from his glove compartment when he heard a car at the edge of the woods and saw his father get out and run toward him. "Didn't you see my note?" he shouted at Mike.

"Yes."

"What did it say?"

"I just told you I saw it."

"It said don't leave, didn't it?"

Mike got the aspirin from his glove compartment while his father stood under the trees, his face white and tense. "All right," Glenn said. "I made a mistake. Good." He shook his head. "Don't scare me like that again." He hurried away, stopped to wait for Mike, then sped up again, toward the motel.

"You said we would talk," Mike said, right behind him. "Just stop and talk to me. Tell me what happened. Then I need to go."

"Fine," his father said. "As soon as we eat. Inez wants us to have a real meal together."

"Why?"

"Who knows?"

And already his father, then Mike, were turning the corner of the motel, with Inez less than ten feet away, unloading plastic grocery sacks from the car. She looked younger in the daylight, and her face was scarred, as if she'd had acne or something worse. "So your dad brought you back," she said cheerfully to Mike. "Good for him. I like company."

"Inez thinks this is a vacation," Glenn said.

"You'd think so, too, if you had my life," Inez said.

Glenn maneuvered both of them into the stale, gloomy cabin, and within just a few minutes there was the sound of a car out front. It didn't occur to Mike to be afraid until he saw his father's reaction. "Inez!" Glenn said. "Go to the window and tell me what you see. Don't stand too close."

"You've got it," Inez said. She moved briskly and watched for almost a minute without speaking.

"Come on!" Glenn said.

"A fat red-haired woman with a little dog, in a beat-up station wagon with Indiana plates. She's checking in."

"Where?"

"Here."

"Which unit, damn it?"

"Don't talk to me like I'm retarded," Inez told him. "The one at the other end."

Glenn looked out the window himself, pulled the curtain closed, and turned toward Mike. "I'm taking a chance, being this close to you. They think I'm dumb enough to be here, and here I am."

"Leave, then," Mike said coldly.

"Don't talk to me like that."

"I hate fighting," Inez said. "It makes me nervous."

"Me, too," Glenn said at once. "I agree with you." He checked the window again. "I'm under a lot of pressure," he told Mike. "I'm asking you to understand that."

"Fine," Mike said. He sat in the armchair and closed his eyes. He repeated to himself the contents of Tom DeWitt's letter. Mike knew more about what the police knew than his father knew he did. That was how he would get through this, he thought. He would stay in control by remembering the knowledge he had.

When he opened his eyes, his father was standing with his arms around Inez. She was so small that she made him look bigger than he was.

"See?" Glenn said. "Everything's fine."

"It's not," Inez said.

"It is. Mike?" he said. "Come tell Inez that everything is okay."

Inez was breathing rapidly, like a panicked animal. Her small eyes were fixed on Mike's face.

"Everything is okay," Mike said. "It's no big deal. I just got mad for a minute."

"See?" Glenn said again.

"No," Inez said.

"Let's eat lunch," Glenn said energetically. "How about it? Anybody hungry?"

"Nobody's hungry," Inez said.

Mike looked at her restless, angry eyes, and at the tension in his father's face. He said that he was hungry.

"Good," Glenn said. "That's what I thought." He patted Inez's arm and filled a pot with water. He put the pot on the stove and turned on the burner. "Simple as could be," he said. "Over and done with." When the water boiled he poured it into three bowls.

"You forgot the ramen noodles!" Inez said.

Glenn laughed loudly. "For Pete's sake," he said. "I did, didn't I? What was I thinking?"

"Get out of here," Inez said in a normal voice. "You men. You don't belong in a kitchen."

Mike and his father grabbed their jackets and went outside. Glenn led Mike around to the back of the motel, from where, on a small rise, they could see through the pines to the stirred-up lake. The clouds were low and dark. The temperature was dropping, and the wind was loud. "Do you understand now what I mean about pressure?" Glenn said to Mike. "There's something wrong with her."

"What?"

"I have no idea." He looked at his footprints in the sandy dirt and slid his feet around, erasing them. "I'll have to leave before too long anyway. She and I have been seen together enough."

"Leave for where?"

"I don't know yet. I can't say."

Inez's intense face appeared around the corner of the building. "Lunch," she said, then disappeared.

"Listen," Mike said. "I want to talk to you. I want to know what happened. But then I have to go back."

"Why?"

"I said I would. And I have studying to do."

"Studying?" Glenn said. "Are you kidding me?"

"It's more than that. What if my roommate tells people I'm missing?"

"Okay, then," Glenn said. "I see what you mean." He checked his watch. "Inez will drive you to a pay phone. You'll call your roommate then."

"No," Mike said.

From inside came the sound of Inez knocking loudly on the wall.

"Let's go," Glenn said. "We have three minutes before she explodes." He was already moving, and Mike, too tired to think quickly enough, too slow to keep up with how fast things were happening, followed at a distance.

INSIDE, they were trapped again at the tiny kitchenette table.

"The soup got cold," Inez said. "While you were out back, telling secrets."

"What secrets?" Glenn said.

"How would I know? You're keeping them from me!" She was laughing, though, and Glenn joined in. Then she turned toward Mike, whose stomach was knotted and tight. "I thought you said you were hungry!"

"I am. It's good." He made himself eat and shook his head when she asked if he wanted more.

"How about cards after lunch?" Glenn said. "Inez is good at cards."

"I specialize in hearts," Inez told Mike.

"Then later on," Glenn said firmly to Mike, "Inez will drive you to a pay phone so that you can call your roommate. How's that, Inez?"

"I like to drive," Inez said.

"You know what we'll do after that?" Glenn said animatedly. "We'll open a bottle of wine. I'll cook the steaks we bought this morning. It's not safe for us to go anywhere as a group. I'm taking a big enough risk staying here one more night."

"Listen," Mike said as politely as he could. "I'll go back to school right after lunch. I don't mind. That way, you and Inez can go someplace safer."

"No," Glenn said. "Seeing you is worth the risk."

"That's more like it," Inez said. "That's how families should be."

TWENTY-SIX

THEY sat on the unmade bed and played hearts. The room was cold, and there had not been more than a minute, since lunch, when Mike and his father had been alone. Inez never sat still. She was like a bird, Mike thought, or like an insect—buzzing from one spot to the next, flinging herself in and out of the bathroom, darting into the kitchenette to light a cigarette at the stove. Mike planned to wait an hour, then tell his father to walk him out to his truck—to talk to him seriously, so that Mike would know exactly what happened. Then Mike would leave.

Meanwhile, a winter storm was moving in. Three inches of snow, they heard on the radio. "Not enough to worry about," Mike's father said, each time Mike got up to look at the threatening sky. "We're lucky. It will keep the police busy."

"No kidding," Inez said, exhaling cigarette smoke. "Imagine no indoor toilet," she told Glenn. "Alton did all the plumbing himself. Can you picture that? As big and crazy as he was?"

"Isn't that something," Glenn said.

She put down her cards and shot into the bathroom. Glenn waited until she closed the door. "Alton was a relative of some kind," he whispered to Mike.

Mike watched the bathroom door. Quietly, he said, "I'm leaving soon. Just so you know. I'm not changing my mind. Whatever you want me to know you can tell me then."

"What do you mean by soon?" Glenn said.

The door flung open. "What's happening soon?" Inez asked.

Glenn hesitated. "Snow," he said then. "I have a feeling. I'm good at predicting things."

"You think you're good at everything," Inez said, and perched on the bed, cross-legged.

They played one more game, then Mike put down his cards. "That's it for me," he said.

"Because you lost," Glenn said. "That's bad strategy. The time to quit is when you're ahead." His eyes were on Inez, who had stood up and was taking small steps from one end of the room to the other.

"I don't like the end of things," she said. "I don't care if it's a card game or a movie. I like things to keep going."

"Get back here and play another hand then," Glenn said with strained lightheartedness. "How about canasta?"

"No," she said. "I don't mean that. You don't get what I mean."

"Sure we do," Glenn said.

"*We* is a lie," Inez said. "It's almost always a lie."

"*I* know what you mean," Glenn said. "That's what I meant to say."

"You can't fix it afterward. I don't know who told you that was fair."

Glenn looked at Mike nervously. He went up to Inez and put his hand on her rough hair, smoothing it back from her small face.

"You don't need to worry about me," Inez said. "You have your loved one here."

"Don't you think I love you?" Glenn whispered. Mike was too close not to hear.

"Of course not. And wouldn't I be in trouble if I did!" She seemed to pull herself together then. She went into the bathroom and came back a moment later, wearing red lipstick. She put on her coat and got her keys. "Who has quarters?" she said matter-of-factly.

It took Mike a second to understand. "I don't need to make a phone call," he said.

"Sure you do," Glenn said.

"I'll go alone then," Mike said. "I mean, I have to get going anyway."

"Make the call," his father said authoritatively. "That way, you can still leave later, if you want to. There's nothing wrong with showing up early. There's only something wrong with showing up late." He took a handful of quarters from his pocket. "Isn't that right?" he said to Inez, who was standing at the door, glowering at Mike.

"Inez?" Glenn said. "What's wrong, honey? Mike didn't mean that he'd rather go alone, did you, Mike? Didn't it come out different than you meant?"

They were both watching him—Inez with fury and his father with desperation or suspicion, Mike didn't know which. He felt unsteady and hot, even in the cold room. The situation had gotten beyond him. "I'm not sure," he said. "I don't know what I meant."

"I told you," Glenn said to Inez. "He's just confused. We've got too much going on here." He picked up Mike's jacket and handed it to him. "Inez loves to drive. I don't know why, but there it is. She wants to take you."

He put an arm around Mike and walked him outside. "You and I will talk when you get back," he said very softly. "Then you can leave. I promise. You're the only person I can tell the truth to." He steered Mike into the passenger seat of the car. In his regular voice he said, "Don't go any farther than you have to. And make the conversation short. People suspect something's wrong when you talk too much."

"Get in," Inez told Mike.

Glenn closed Mike's door and hurried inside. When Mike looked back, the road was empty except for the station wagon at the far end. Mike hadn't seen either the woman or the dog go in or out.

All right, Mike thought, as Inez started driving. He'd

been manipulated into this car ride because he hadn't been smart enough to avoid it; he hadn't been smart enough because he was overtired, plus whatever it was that was wrong with his stomach. As things were now, he thought, it was easier just to make the call—to go along with most of what his father wanted—then leave afterward.

Inez lit a cigarette. "Are you okay then with your dad?" she asked. "Children should never be angry at their parents. Your father's not responsible for what he does."

"Why not?"

"He's a man," Inez said. "He's no more responsible than you are."

Snow was beginning to fall. Inez reduced her speed, driving with exaggerated care. Along the road were flat brown fields and fenced pastures. There were few cars on the road besides theirs.

"I was in a terrible accident once," Inez said. "I almost lost someone I love."

"Who?"

"Me," she said. "Inez."

"Why do you like to drive, then?"

"That's a good question," Inez said. "I'm going to give that some thought."

They drove for fifteen silent minutes before approaching a small town—a boarded-up elementary school and a closed gas station. "Hicksville," Inez said. Further on was a grain elevator, a diner, and a stretch of modest houses. Inez stopped at a Handy-Mart that had a pay phone out front.

She got out with Mike and stood next to him at the phone. "I like fresh air," she said. "I'm not like your dad, the way he holes himself up." She opened her purse and took out three dollars' worth of quarters.

"I have a calling card," Mike said.

Inez laughed. "And you're in college!" She pressed the change into his hand. "Go ahead and call. It's cold out here."

Mike dialed his phone number and put in the quarters. Nobody answered. When the phone machine came on, he said, "Raymond? It's Mike. I might not come back tonight. I might come back tomorrow."

"Right," Inez whispered. She lit a fresh cigarette and peered into the store window as Mike hung up the phone. "Is there anything you need?" she asked. "Any personal grooming items?"

"No."

"Magazines? A *Playboy*?"

"No, thanks."

She seemed reluctant to leave.

"Is there something you want?" Mike asked.

"Not really. Not anything they have."

She stood there a moment longer, her face close to the glass, her breath creating small foggy circles. Then she and Mike got back in the car and she pulled onto the windswept road, the houses and patchy grass alongside it dusted with snow. "Do you like malls?" Inez asked.

"Not much."

"I knew you'd say that." Her voice was sad. "I like walking through them. I like the way they smell. I like the way the lights look." She glanced over at him. She touched his knee with her fingers. "Do you know what I mean?"

"Not exactly."

"Well," she said. "At least you're honest. That's more than I can say for you-know-who." She turned on the radio and found only static. She turned it off and sang, " 'Hello, window. Is that a tear I see in the corner of your pane?' "

"Willie Nelson," Mike said.

"That's right. Score one for you."

There was more snow on the road now, and she was sitting forward in the seat, driving intently. When they were close to the turnoff for the motel, she said, "Why didn't you want to go with me? What's wrong with my company?"

Mike's stomach hurt again. "Nothing," he said. "It just seemed easier that way."

"Easier for you," Inez said. "Isn't that a surprise."

TWENTY-SEVEN

THE cabin door opened as soon as Mike and Inez got out of the car. "How did it go?" Glenn said. He came toward them in the snow. It was dusk by then; there was a light on in the cabin and one at the far end of the motel.

"Fine," Inez stated. She slammed the car door and stomped past him.

"Everything went smoothly?" Glenn said, talking fast.

"What did I just say?" Inez said.

"Isn't she a good driver, Mike? I told you that. She's nice and careful."

Mike was standing in the road, halfway between the car and the motel, waiting for his father to walk toward him and for Inez to go inside. But she didn't go inside. She stopped in the open doorway. "Get the wine out," she told Glenn.

"Okay. Great," Glenn said. "Come on," he said to Mike. "Come in out of the snow."

Mike spoke as cautiously and judiciously as he could, for Inez's benefit, not for his father's. He understood now that everything depended on her reactions. "I thought I would leave now," he said. "That way I won't get home too late. I thought we could talk for a minute. Then I'll take off."

Inez scowled at Mike. "He doesn't want to be around me," she told Glenn.

"That's not true," Glenn said. "That doesn't sound like Mike."

"Who does it sound like then?" Inez said icily.

"Nobody," Glenn said. "That doesn't sound like anybody I know. Right, Mike?"

Mike looked toward the far end of the motel, where the station wagon was parked. What if he walked down there? he thought suddenly. Would it scare his father into doing what he wanted? What if it didn't? But Mike was too worn-out to think beyond that. Meanwhile, Inez's small eyes were fastened on his face.

"Mike?" his father said. "Let's have one glass of wine and eat dinner. Are you a drinker these days? Then you can be on your way. A glass of wine won't hurt you as long as you eat."

"He doesn't want to be here!" Inez shouted, and Mike's father flinched.

"Let's talk inside, Mike," he said urgently, looking up and down the road. "Look at us, standing in the cold like fools."

"Don't call me names!" Inez said. "Call yourself whatever you want, but leave me out of it!"

"Mike, please," his father said, moving toward him. "Just to get her inside," he whispered. "Please. So she doesn't leave with the car."

"What?" Inez said loudly.

"Just one more hour," his father pleaded.

INSIDE, Glenn poured wine into three plastic glasses. He clinked his own glass against Inez's without making a toast, and he and Inez drank theirs quickly. "So everything went smoothly," he said to her. "I knew it would. I knew I could count on you."

"You don't know anything," Inez said. But with her next drink the anger went out of her voice; she poured Glenn a second glass, and topped off Mike's, where he stood next to the window, wearing his jacket. "Take that thing off," she said. "Can't you tell it's warmed up in here?"

"I fixed the heater while you were gone," Glenn told her, his voice no longer sounding so lively. Mike watched the two of them—the way Inez moved rapidly and his father navigated warily around her. Mike told himself that all he had to do was be careful around Inez, to make sure she stayed. That was one thing his father was right about. Otherwise the only person there with a vehicle would be Mike. That would have occurred to him sooner if he'd had more sleep, if he'd felt healthy the way he used to, a long time ago. He looked out the window at the snow, and at dusk turning into night.

In the kitchenette Inez was pouring herself a third glass of wine. "Go for it," his father said, and she reached out and put her hand on his crotch. He jumped away. "Oh," she said, laughing. "You didn't mean that?"

Glenn turned back to the stove. He stopped smiling. He looked so intense that Mike was afraid something was happening to him—a stroke or a heart attack.

"Dad?" he said, using that word for the first time since he'd gotten there.

"What?"

"Nothing. Never mind."

Then dinner was ready, and though Mike had stopped drinking, his father and Inez hadn't. "I'm glad you're here," Glenn told Mike at the table. "Inez understands that you have to leave soon, and I know this has been tough on you. But now you can see how it's been for me. I wanted you to see it from my perspective."

"What's this 'it' you're talking about?" Inez said. She gestured with her arm and knocked Glenn's wineglass off the table.

"Goddamn it," he said angrily. "Can't we have one meal where nobody spills anything?"

Mike hadn't heard his father say that in years. It was what he'd said whenever Mike had spilled anything as a child. How often could that have happened? Mike thought now. How irritating could it have been?

Inez had stopped eating. "Who the hell spilled anything at lunch?" she said, her voice cold and dangerous-sounding.

"I don't know," Glenn said. "Somebody."

"Nobody," Inez said.

"Mike did, didn't he?"

"No." She got up from the table and stood in front of the small stove. She lit a cigarette from the gas burner.

"Don't smoke while we're eating," Glenn said. "I've told you that before. I hate that."

"I don't care what you hate."

Mike stood up, sick and dizzy. "Just back off," he said to his father.

"I've been backing off," Glenn said. "I think that's obvious."

"I think that's obvious," Inez said. She walked up behind him and stubbed out her cigarette in his food.

Mike's father crossed the room and opened the front door. He shut it hard behind him.

"There he goes," Inez said. "Into the cold without a jacket. If that isn't crazy." She lit another cigarette and sat down at the table. "You haven't eaten a thing," she said to Mike. "That's a good steak you're wasting."

Mike, the cigarette smoke in his face, hurried into the bathroom, vomited, then sat on the floor with his head down, his hands cold with sweat. He tried to picture himself four hundred miles away, in Wheatley. He imagined driving out to Crow Lake, lying down on the front seat of his truck, and letting himself sleep.

"Mike?" Inez said. She pounded on the bathroom door. "I don't see him. I don't know what happened to him." She banged on the door until he opened it and came out.

"It's too dark to see anything," he told her.

"No. That's wrong. I can see the car." She opened the front door. "Glenn?" she called. She waited a moment. "He's not answering. Maybe he's too far away."

"That's probably it," Mike said. Inez looked at him hatefully. "I'm agreeing with you," he said. "I'm saying you're probably right."

She opened the door again. "Glenn!" she shouted into the night.

"Listen," Mike said. "Don't yell like that. Come inside." He touched her arm; when she stepped back in he pulled the door shut. "It's okay," he told her. "He'll come back. He'll walk in here in just a few minutes."

"He was done with his food!" she said in a high-pitched voice. "I was just putting garbage into garbage!"

"Maybe he wasn't done," Mike said. "Maybe he had a little steak left on his plate."

"That was your plate, with that nice steak left over! I don't know why you don't eat what's put in front of you!" She opened the door again. "Glenn?" she called tenderly. "Come back in, honey. Warm yourself up." She crossed her arms. She turned around and faced Mike. "Why does he want to make me so unhappy? What is he punishing me for?"

"The cigarette," Mike said softly. He watched her face

change from distraught to hopeless. She closed the door and sat down on the thin, worn carpeting. It's all right, Mike wanted to tell her. People get over being mad. People walk out and then they come back. But he couldn't say anything. Like her, he watched the door.

TWENTY-EIGHT

THE room was too warm now, and there seemed to be no way to adjust the heat. The kitchenette was cluttered with dirty dishes and pots, the bed had not been made nor the sleeping bag rolled up. Inez had not moved. She was sitting with her knees pulled up, making small, moaning sounds, and Mike thought that he should try to comfort her. But he was afraid that she'd use it as a reason to get crazier, even. He stayed where he was, his stomach hurting, looking at the wallpaper behind her. It was yellowed and old. Everything in the cabin was discolored. Probably nothing had ever been nice. If you weren't depressed when you walked in, you'd want to kill yourself by the time you left.

"Look," Mike said. "I'll see if I can find him."

The snow was falling less heavily, and Mike walked far into the field across the road, then back and behind the motel, where he and his father had stood earlier. He felt better being outside in the cold darkness. The wind was decreasing, and an owl was calling from somewhere behind him. The pine boughs were blanketed lightly with snow.

"Glenn," he said softly, as an experiment, to see how strange it felt to say the name. But it seemed even stranger to say "Dad"—because his father never had been one, really, he knew, not the kind they showed in movies and Father's Day commercials. And even if those were phony, his father still hadn't been one in Mike's own mind.

He stood in back of the motel, breathing the cold air, knowing that he didn't want to find him. Because he'd gotten where he was on his own. He'd managed this far without him.

In the next moment there were footsteps and voices, and his father and Inez were hurrying toward him. "I didn't know where you were," Glenn said, panting. "Inez wouldn't tell me."

"Fuck you," Inez said.

"Come on now. Don't be like that. I'm here now."

She gave him a black look, then vanished; Glenn—with Mike following only because he was sick again suddenly—ran after her to the front of the cabin and inside, where she was furiously throwing her belongings into a small flowered bag.

"I was at fault," Glenn said. "I know that. I made a mistake." He pursued her into the kitchenette. "Tell me what you want me to say!"

"How about nothing?" Inez said. "How does that sound?" She zipped up her overnight bag and put on her coat. She was out the door, with Glenn running after her, when Mike got past them to the bathroom.

By the time he came out, his father was standing at the open door, alone. The car was gone. Mike thought he saw movement at the other end of the motel, near the station wagon, but whatever he thought he saw was gone when he looked again.

Behind him now, his father was packing. "She'll be back in a few minutes," he said. "But I won't wait more than ten. Then we'll have to get in your truck and leave." He was throwing things into the duffel bag Mike had taken to summer camp ten years earlier. For a second Mike could think only of standing in that clearing, watching his mother help his weeping father into the car. Inside the duffel bag his mother had left a note: "Try not to be homesick. We'll be back for you in two weeks."

"Where are your keys?" his father said. "Let me have them just in case."

"In case what?" Mike said.

"In case anything happens." He got out a plastic trash bag and threw everything in the kitchenette into it: dirty dishes, leftover food, the contents of the refrigerator. Then he put on a pair of gloves and cleaned off every surface in the room with a wet towel. "Isn't this something?" he said to Mike. "Doesn't this remind you of the movies we used to watch?"

Mike shook his head.

"Get your things together. What did you bring?"

"Nothing."

"Then watch the window for me."

Mike put his cold hands against the cold glass, watching for Inez's car. If she would just come back, he thought, he could walk out the minute he saw her headlights. He could walk out and be in his truck, driving away, in less than five minutes. He could leave, even if he didn't find out anything from his father, as long as his father had somebody else to turn to.

Glenn put the duffel bag and trash bag next to the door. "Do you have any money?" he asked Mike.

Mike gave him thirty dollars—all but five of what he had.

"Good," Glenn said. "Where are your keys?"

"I have them."

"Give them to me. I'll drive. I don't mind. It will look less suspicious than you driving me."

"Driving you where?" Mike said.

"I'm not sure yet. Maybe Cleveland." He switched off the light and came toward Mike. He held out his hand.

"Give her more time," Mike said. "You said she'd come back. You said you were helping her."

"She's crazy."

"But not completely!"

"Okay," his father said. "Forget Cleveland. I can make do with Minneapolis. We can be there in two hours."

"She'll be back before then!"

"Just give me the keys. I'm only asking this one thing. After Minneapolis, you can turn around and drive back to school." His thin face was tightly pale. "If you didn't want to help me," he said, "you shouldn't have come."

Mike stepped back from his father then. He looked at the hand he held out—first for money, and now for this, which Mike should have realized from the beginning.

"I want to know what happened," Mike said. "I want to know why you did what you did."

His father glared at him. "She grabbed my arm," he said. "I never intended to shoot her. It was at least sixty percent her fault. Because she was like you are now," he told Mike fiercely. "She was going to leave me when I needed her."

LEAVING, and leaving his father in the cabin, alone, wasn't as hard to do as Mike had thought. He just opened the door. But behind him his father was crying. His shoulders were hunched and his arms were loose at his sides. Tears were streaming down his face into his collar.

Mike went into the bathroom for Kleenex. Standing in front of the sink, in the harsh brightness of the overhead light, he stared at his own face in the mirror. It was just a sound, he told himself, and after a while it would stop. It wasn't going to kill him to hear it, no matter how bad it made him feel.

He delivered the Kleenex to his father, who followed

Mike outside and down the dirt road to the rutted path
leading into the woods. Mike wanted to stop and explain
that there were things you couldn't make people do—even
people who loved you. But he kept walking instead, and by
the time he unlocked his truck, his father was twenty feet
behind him, standing without a jacket in the middle of the
snow-covered trail. Mike drove out slowly, watching his father move aside, finally, letting him go.

MIKE drove for thirty minutes before stopping to call
Tom DeWitt from a pay phone outside a closed gas station.
He dialed the third number, the one that was cellular, and
hoped that it would just keep ringing. He was willing to
stand all night in the cold, listening to it ring. But Tom
answered. "We know," he said. "Don't say anything. We're
at the motel now."

Mike held the receiver, looking at the road and snow and
at his blue truck, parked safely in the darkness.

"Where are you?" Tom said, and Mike told him the name
of the gas station, and the town it was close to. "Stay there,"
he told Mike. "Just sit in your truck until I get there."

Mike, waiting in the darkness, already knew most of
what Tom would tell him later: that the red-haired woman
at the motel was a police officer, and that there were more
police with her; that they had listened in on Glenn's call to
Mike at school and had followed Mike before that, in
Brookings; and that Tom had been in Brookings, too, more

than once. And, most important of all, that Tom's letter had correctly predicted that Glenn would contact Mike, would try to involve him.

Mike had been too worried about himself—that was what he thought now. He should have been smarter about that letter. He should have believed it more, and he should have trusted his father less. He should have said no when he called. He should have done nothing. Because Tom De-Witt would have caught his father soon enough anyway, without him.

TWENTY minutes later Mike saw headlights, coming fast. Then Tom was getting into Mike's truck, his heavy jacket swinging open to reveal a shoulder holster and gun. His face was chapped from the wind. "Are you all right?" he asked.

"Tell me what happened."

"Your father's under arrest. He's all right, not injured in any way." He settled himself into the seat and pulled his jacket closed, over the gun. "You're in the clear," he told Mike. "The important thing is that you didn't help him. All that matters in the end is what you do."

Mike watched him brush snow from his hair and jacket—as if he'd been out hunting just deer, Mike thought. "Does that go for you, too?" he said bitterly. "Is that why you feel so good now?"

"Who said I felt good?"

"Don't you?"

"It's not that simple," Tom said. "Sometimes you regret things you have to do. Sometimes you can't find another way to do them."

"So you screw people over."

Three state police cars went by, heading west, one after the other, the headlights shining in sequence into the cab of Mike's truck. "My dad?" Mike said, and Tom nodded. They both watched the cars for as long as they could see them.

"Sometimes you screw yourself, too," Tom said, in a less certain voice. "Not usually, but when you want to stay in touch with people afterward."

"My mother?"

"You *and* your mother."

Mike looked at the dark, empty highway. For the first time he knew something significant that Tom didn't: It wasn't Tom DeWitt Mike's mother cared for. But Mike didn't feel even glad. He looked at Tom's weathered face and his thinning hair, and felt bad for him.

"I haven't called your mother yet," Tom said. "I wanted to wait until you were away from here. But I'll be honest with her. I'm not asking you to keep our surveillance of you secret."

"But you'd like to."

"Would it do any good if I did?" He smiled at Mike without looking happy. "Yes. I would like to. But I won't."

"What was the point of the dog, at the motel?" Mike asked quietly. "Whose dog was that?"

"It was just a prop," Tom said. "Your dad likes dogs. He doesn't think of them suspiciously."

"Do you plan everything you do?" Mike said. "Don't you ever do anything by accident? I mean, just by chance?"

Tom thought before he spoke. "Yes," he said. Then, "No. Probably not. Not for a long time." He zipped up his jacket and said, "I'll call you in a few days. I'll tell you whatever I can. Meanwhile, go back to school. Go to your classes. The worst has already happened."

"Because of us," Mike said.

"No. Because of what your father did." Tom looked at Mike for a few seconds. Then, hesitantly, as if he weren't sure what Mike might do, he rested a strong hand on his shoulder. "Be careful driving back to Brookings," he told him, then opened the door and stepped out into the cold.

TWENTY-NINE

MIKE stayed there for a long time after Tom left. He noticed, without thinking about it, that the snow had stopped and that a quarter moon was visible. And he noticed that now, because of the moon, he could see farther into the pasture across the road than he'd been able to before. But he didn't feel much of anything. The part of him that had been preoccupied with his father was now vacant, just emptied out. There was nothing else inside of him, he thought. Next to him on the seat was the card with Tom's phone numbers on it, and Mike picked it up and put it in the glove compartment, out of sight.

Finally he just started driving. Two miles east of the state line, remembering about the license plate, he turned into a parking lot next to a church. He drove to the back of it, where the snow was untouched, and as he replaced the

Minnesota plate with his South Dakota one, he remembered his father saying, "I don't believe there's a God. Not
many people are brave enough to say that."

That struck Mike now as a foolish thing to say. But what
did he, himself, believe in? He didn't know. He looked at
the small cemetery next to the church, a layer of snow as
thin as paper on top of the gray stones. He put on his seat
belt when he got back in his truck.

He drove mile after mile through the darkness. Then,
his stomach still queasy, he stopped near the interstate and
bought a 7-Up at an all-night convenience store.

"I guess the snow's stopped," said the short, older
woman behind the counter. "That was the earliest snow I
can remember in a lot of years."

"Me, too," Mike said.

"You're too young to know what a lot of years means,"
she told him.

A man in a cowboy hat came in just before Mike left. "I
guess the snow's stopped," the woman said to him. "That
was the earliest snow I can remember in a lot of years."

That should have made Mike smile, at least, but he
barely registered it. He walked to his truck, got in, and
pulled onto the flat, straight highway that would take him
into Brookings. He drove automatically and not very carefully. He realized that there was something wrong with
the way he felt. He should have been having some specific
reaction, he thought, like relief, if nothing else. But he
couldn't say that he felt relieved. What he did know was

that he was tired and cold. He never, maybe, had been that tired.

He turned on the radio and listened to a country station: songs about love of one kind or another. There was a commercial for the Corn Palace, in Mitchell. Mike had been there with his parents, but Donetta had never seen it. "My father was going to take me," she'd told Mike more than once. "It was on his 'things-to-do-next-summer' list."

Unexpectedly, the sadness of that affected him, and made him see what he hadn't seen before. There were too many things on that list. Donetta had named nine or ten over the years since her father had died. He never would have done any of them, Mike understood now. Summers would have come and gone, and all he would have done was kept writing them down.

Close to Brookings now, watching the highway, Mike started to cry. Tears, unaccompanied at first by emotion, ran down his face, and when he no longer could see the road he pulled off to the side of the highway and wept. It was the only time he ever had. Hearing that word Mike would have thought that he knew what it meant, but he wouldn't have known that it was like this. Tears were only salt water, Donetta's father had said, but he had been wrong about that, too. What they were made of, Mike knew now, didn't tell you what they did. They brought up to the surface what you had pushed down to the bottom. They let you know how much of you there was.

It was a while before they stopped. Then he wiped his

face with the sleeve of his jacket and looked out at the flat, open land along the highway. He was homesick for the fields near Wheatley. He was homesick for the Black Hills, from where he had taken the high, narrow roads that led down to the outskirts of Wheatley. From the Black Hills he had seen, sort of, himself. He didn't know yet how he would get that back.

IN Brookings, he drove down the empty streets to Hansen Hall and parked behind it, next to his motorcycle. The lobby was deserted except for a couple making out on a couch in a dark corner. Mike tiredly climbed the stairs. Raymond was asleep, though he woke up when Mike came in. "I thought you weren't coming back until tomorrow," he said.

"I changed my mind."

"Why?"

"No reason," Mike said. Then he said, painfully, "No. There is one. But it's too much to explain. I'll tell you to-morrow."

He went down to the rest room, returned, and locked the door behind him. He undressed and got into bed. For the most part, the dorm was quiet. He heard a door slam, then the sighing sound of the heat coming on, which stirred the curtains. He could see the outline of his desk and chair, and the shapes of his books—the familiarity of things that belonged to him.

Across from him Raymond yawned and turned over. "Your girlfriend called," he said.

"Did she?"

"Twice."

Mike lay on his back in the darkness, picturing his father's face, and the three state police cars going past, one after the other, after the other. Too many things had happened. Too many of them had revolved around Mike. But that was over now.

And gradually, without effort, as Mike let himself move toward sleep, he realized that whatever happened to his father was not connected to him. There weren't unbreakable strings between people in families. Mike had thought there were, but when his father had pulled on them too hard, had counted on them unfairly, they'd broken.

He closed his eyes. He thought about driving up into the Black Hills on the curving roads; about his bedroom at home, with its view of the Hylers' house across the street; and about the Hylers' cats—the outside ones—waiting patiently on the broken-down porch for their dinners.

And finally he reached for his Walkman and headphones and listened to the tape Donetta had made for him. The first thing on the cassette was her voice. "It's three o'clock in the morning," she said. "I can't sleep, I can't dream, and I can't stop thinking of you."

He rewound and rewound it, listening to her voice until he fell asleep.

ABOUT THE AUTHOR

Judy Troy was born in northern Indiana. She has taught writing at an alternative high school, Indiana University, and the University of Missouri. Her collection of stories, *Mourning Doves,* was nominated for a *Los Angeles Times* Book Award, and she received the 1996 Whiting Writers' Award. She is now Alumni-Writer-in-Residence at Auburn University.

ABOUT THE TYPE

This book was set in Garamond No. 3, a variation of the classic Garamond typeface originally designed by the Parisian type cutter Claude Garamond (1480–1561).

Claude Garamond's distinguished romans and italics first appeared in *Opera Ciceronis* in 1543–44. The Garamond types are clear, open, and elegant.